PRAISE FOR
WHERE ANGELS PREY

"*Where Angels Prey* is an engaging and touching story of the collision of altruism and aspiration. Its narration of how the Indian rural poor suffer from this collision, in the context of the spectacular growth and equally spectacular crisis of the Andhra Pradesh microfinance industry, shocks and moves. I found it a most enjoyable, but also most disturbing, read!"

Matthew Gamser, *CEO, SME Finance Forum, International Finance Corporation, Washington DC, USA*

"During the very spectacular implosion of microfinance in Andhra Pradesh in 2010, Ramesh Arunachalam was merciless in his analysis. Combining field trips, secondary research and his experience in the rural development space, he stripped bare the malaise in the sector. It is excellent that he has now parsed all that knowhow into this racy entertaining novel."

M Rajshekhar, *Senior Journalist, Scroll.in and former Senior Assistant Editor (Rural India, Environment), The Economic Times*

"This novel is a brilliant piece of work from a person who has seen at close quarters the microfinance industry's rise and fall in Andhra Pradesh. The plot, fit for a movie, is beautifully woven into all the happenings that have plagued the sector. It makes for such a compelling read that it can't be put down even once!"

Madhusudhan Lagisetty, *Assistant Vice President, Tata AIG Life Insurance Co Ltd*

"Money is trust encrypted; the story of how it can be used to destroy trust in the name of the poor is vividly portrayed in this highly entertaining book...the title says it all."

Al Fernandez, *Chairman NABFINS Ltd and*
Padmashree Awardee 2000

"Where Angels Prey is art imitating life ... a great read the first and the second time around."

Jami Solli, *Executive Director of the Global Alliance*
for Legal Aid (GALA), USA

"Really enjoyed the novel *Where Angels Prey....* Its unique plot and fast pace make it a very entertaining and smooth read."

Prof M S Sriram, *formerly Professor at IIM (Ahmedabad) and*
currently Visiting Professor at IIM (Bangalore)

"Where Angels Prey is wonderfully written and captivating. I thought I'd read a chapter, but the narrative was so gripping I went through the whole book at one stretch."

V Ramamurthy, *I.A.S. (Retd), 1959 Batch*

"Where *Angels Prey* pulls and absorbs you into its plot and holds you there from start to finish."

Joy Deshmukh-Ranadive, *Global Head, Corporate Social*
Responsibility, Tata Consultancy Services

"A Brilliant Read—*Where Angels Prey* blurs the line between fiction and truth. From a man who understands money as well as anyone I know, this book paints the two worlds that wrestle in India in the 21st century. Descriptive, taut, with well-etched-out characters, and most importantly entertaining. This book is crying out to be made into a film!"

Anshuman Jha, *Actor*

"Riveting.... Designed to be the ideal solution to meet the financial needs of the poor, somewhere the microfinance sector decided to change course to be in the commercial, profit-making zone, placing millions of lives at the risk of failure and complete bankruptcy. Many sector leaders became the same demons, if not worse, that they swore to slay. The book beautifully highlights the interconnectedness of issues and actors, helping the reader analyse the situation on the ground and questioning many of the so-called 'accepted' truths. Congratulations to Ramesh for having successfully converted his long-standing experience with the sector into a gripping narrative that will have readers asking for much more."

Moutushi Sengupta, *Director–India,*
MacArthur Foundation

"From rural Andhra Pradesh to the shiny lobbies of Wall Street, this financial thriller is a must read for everybody. Don't worry if you're not familiar with microfinance because Ramesh Arunachalam breaks down the concepts and the scams associated with microfinance in this entertaining saga. This book boasts of Arunachalam's sheer brilliance as a writer and as a financial expert. Smooth, fast and nail-biting! I wonder when the movie is going to be out!"

Anand Bhaskar, *Musician*

"Fantastic storyline, but startlingly realistic; written racily, yet in impeccable English. Interweaving fact and fiction, this novel is a creative and compelling read."

G R Swaminathan,
Assistant Solicitor General of India

"No one doubted the power of microfinance in pulling millions out of poverty. But, a spate of suicides by the borrowers in 2010 raised more questions than answers. For an inside story of what happened and why, you don't need to go farther than this *brilliant yet entertaining novel*, which is so hard to put down. Ramesh's idea to write the microfinance story as fiction is ingenious. The intrigue behind the rise and fall of the sector could be brought out no holds barred. It's a must read. Like one of the characters in the book said, 'We owe it to them—to each of those fifty plus people who have been robbed of their lives, and to the hundreds of thousands of others whose trust has been violated'."

S Sivakumar, *Architect, ITC e-Choupal*

"*Where Angels Prey* is really an excellent read! This graphic exploration of the once universally-lauded microfinance industry is bang on target. It works not just as a great read but as something to make you think a little deeper along the way. Written with flair, verve and a superb eye for detail—which is not surprising as Arunachalam is India's leading microfinance analyst—this gripping novel is a trip into the darker side of the poverty industry as it rampages and careens through the lives of the poor under cover of actually helping them. I look forward to the film in due course—it will be India's very own 'Wall Street'!"

Milford J. B. Bateman *PhD, Freelance consultant on local economic development, Visiting Professor of Economics, Juraj Dobrila at Pula University, Croatia and Adjunct Professor of Development Studies, St Marys University, Halifax, Canada*

"This rip-roaring piece of fiction races the reader through the halls of the Mumbai and New York Stock exchanges and into the villages of Andhra Pradesh. *Where Angels Prey* exposes the worst of what can happen when commercial interests and desperation collide: a train wreck tragic in every way. At the heart of the story, as two journalists work unstoppably to interpret a rain of motives, they uncover why and how the angels prey."

Kim Wilson, *Faculty, The Fletcher School, Tufts University*

Where Angels Prey

Ramesh S Arunachalam

First published in India in 2015 by:
Ramesh S Arunachalam
rameshsa2009@gmail.com

Print Book Indian Edition ISBN: 9789384439347
Print Book International Edition ISBN: 9789384439378
eBook ISBN: 9789384439361

Publishing facilitation: AuthorsUpFront
Cover design: PealiDezine
Typeset in Warnock Pro by Ram Das Lal, New Delhi (NCR)

This book, *Where Angels Prey*, is a work of FICTION loosely inspired by events that took place in the microfinance sector in India and also other parts of the world. Therefore, the names, characters, businesses, places, institutions and incidents are primarily the product of the author's imagination and resemblance (if any) to actual persons, living or dead, or actual institutions is purely coincidental. This book of FICTION does NOT purport to be a direct representation and/ or depiction of any particular individual/MFI/institution in India or elsewhere, existing or past.

Contents

PROLOGUE

Is the man ever going to stop?

Renuka surreptitiously looks out of the window in an attempt to distract herself from the unintelligible drone of the rather distinguished looking speaker at the head of the room. Her English vocabulary is rather basic, a grand total of four words that include *bank, loan, meeting* and *thanks*. A fact that the speaker is either unaware of or is possibly indifferent to. The sights on the road below seem more interesting if only in their contrast to the rarefied atmosphere of the room. Here she is, seated on the fourteenth floor of the gleaming skyscraper that houses the Bombay Stock Exchange, looking down at the shiny tin roofs of the slum tenements below, the dirt and grime a sharp contrast to the affluence on display around her. Pavement dwellers conduct their morning ablutions right on the street and blank-eyed children try to make a quick rupee cleaning the windows of the fancy cars that crawl by, as the owners wave them away like they were pesky flies.

All this seems such a far cry from the little village Renuka comes from and where her family have lived for generations. She now longs to be back there, enveloped by the open spaces and the sounds of her village. The early morning crowing of the roosters seems so far removed from the honking and bustle of this big city. She looks wearily at her companions and wonders if they feel as disoriented and lost as she does. She huddles closer to them, desperate to draw some courage from their proximity. She can almost sense the collective thought, uppermost in all their minds.

"How did I get here?"

All the women wear saris in the traditional way with the *pallu* hooked over their left shoulders and covering their heads. Their gaudily coloured clothes and betel juice-stained teeth stand out in comparison to the sober shades that the gentry around them are attired in. It is evident to all that they do not belong here. Even when dressed in their Sunday best! There aren't too many other women in the room apart from the few female reporters, who look so sophisticated in their pant-suits and make-up that she feels even more intimidated by them than by the men.

Renuka herself has had no formal education, nor has her husband. The family owns half an acre of barren land with no irrigation facilities. As a result, the couple hire themselves out as agricultural labour. The supplementary income that accrues from selling the milk from her cows has helped to ensure that her three girls go to a private school where they are taught to speak English. Renuka can't help but wistfully hope that their daughters grow up to be like these other women, educated and with well-paying jobs, rather than suffer their mother's lot in life.

Renuka tries to discreetly nudge Gangamma.

"How much longer?"

"How would I know?" Gangamma whispers back.

Renuka tries hard not to squirm. The air-conditioning is not helping.

"It's cold...I need to go!"

Bommakka glares at them both. She is a little bit older and has always been the leader among them. She has studied up to Class 10, which makes her highly educated as compared to the rest of them. She was married off at the age of 16 and had borne four children by the time she was 20. Tired and exhausted, she finally took herself to a free clinic and underwent a tubectomy to prevent further pregnancies. After regaining her strength, she took over the family finances and rallied the women around her to take control of their lives as well. She had a positive spirit which helped her make things happen for herself and for others around her too, so much so that even people older than her tended to look to her for guidance. It was she who had convinced the men-folk to allow their wives to board a plane, saying that it was good for their community and their village. She came from a long line of storytellers who passed down legends through the ages, which helped her find the words to state her case eloquently.

Despite all that, Bommakka had been as taken aback the first time they saw a plane at close quarters. As for Renuka, whenever she spotted a plane that appeared like a speck in the distant skies, she would wonder how normal-sized people actually fit into them! Did they feed people some magic potion to shrink them enough to fit into those tiny planes?

Ramulamma, the hundred-year-old hunchback of Madiseri village, had warned her so. Renuka promised her that she would refuse all the food and drink offered to her on the way. Thankfully, the plane was not as small as she had thought. It could accommodate not just her but also her nine other friends, Bommakka, Sir Garu, Nagalakshmi madam, and a couple of hundred other people.

A round of polite applause interrupts her thoughts.

She is relieved to see Annayya Garu stand up. This means that the meeting is over.

"Renuka, take this!"

Renuka looks curiously at the object that he holds out to her. It is a fat wooden stick. What does she have to do now? Nagalakshmi Madam smiles encouragingly at her.

"Hit it!"

Renuka looks in the direction that she is pointing towards. It is a large, round iron plate.

"Announce to the world the beginning of a new era!"

Renuka hits the gong with all her might. She does not know that she is ringing the opening bell for trading at the Bombay Stock Exchange. She is just a little pawn in a much larger game which she is yet to grasp.

The sound reverberates across the room. The stock of SAMMAAN Microfinance is now officially listed on the Bombay Stock Exchange. A company providing financial services to the poor is now rubbing shoulders with the rich and mighty of corporate India!

"It is Destination NYSE next! Westward Ho!" Annayya Garu exclaims with great cheer.

Renuka has no clue what he is talking about and wonders if her cow back home in the village has delivered its calf already.

CHAPTER 1

NEW YORK, 5 SEPTEMBER 2010

President Obama looks suitably sombre as he speaks to the camera. Bob can see the lines on his face and how much this presidency has aged him. He tries to pay attention to the speech even as he wonders how the President can so passionately repeat the same things over and over....

I ran for President because for much of the last decade, a very specific governing philosophy had reigned about how America should work: Cut taxes, especially for millionaires and billionaires. Cut regulations for special interests. Cut trade deals even if they didn't benefit our workers. Cut back on investments in our people and in our future—in education and clean energy, in research and technology. The idea was that if we just had blind faith in the market, if we let corporations play by their own rules, if we left everyone else to fend for themselves, that America would grow and America would prosper.

And for a time this idea gave us the illusion of prosperity.

*We saw financial firms and CEOs take in record profits
and record bonuses. We saw a housing boom that led to
new home owners and new jobs in construction. Consumers
bought more condos and bigger cars and better TVs.*

*But while all this was happening, the broader economy
was becoming weaker. Nobody understands that more than
the people of Ohio. Job growth between 2000 and 2008 was
slower than it had been in any economic expansion since
World War II—slower than it's been over the last year. The
wages and incomes of middle-class families kept falling while
the cost of everything from tuition to health care kept on
going up. Folks were forced to put more debt on their credit
cards and borrow against homes that many couldn't afford
to buy in the first place. And meanwhile, a failure to pay
for two wars and two tax cuts for the wealthy helped turn a
record surplus into a record deficit.*

By now, Bob is finding it a challenge to keep his eyes open.
Blame it on the lunch of roast beef and potatoes, flavoured
with *garam masala* to give it an Indian twist. The drone of the
TV only adds to the drowsiness. Bob gently rubs his hand over
his over-stuffed stomach, wondering if he has time for a quick
nap. A senior economics correspondent with *The New York
Post*, Robert Bradlee's high pressure job and erratic schedule
have turned sleep into a luxury to be grabbed whenever the
opportunity presents itself. There is also the pressure of an
evolving personal relationship that he is determined to give
his best to. His mouth curves into a smile at the thought of
Priya, his girlfriend of over a year. A Fulbright scholar from
Hyderabad in India, she is doing her postdoctoral research in
development economics at Columbia University. They had

met at the opening of a highly recommended play that Bob's friend had dragged him to. After dating for over six months, they had decided to take their relationship to the next level and Priya moved in with him. Even while taking the plunge, both had their reservations over the advisedness of the move. Priya had a bad marriage in her past, while Bob had always thought of himself as commitment-phobic. Surprisingly for both of them, the arrangement worked out pretty smoothly and their time together had been both harmonious and happy.

Priya's voice cuts through his pleasant reverie; she asks if he would like ice-cream for dessert. He wonders how his beautiful Indian friend could be so perky after that massive meal. She loves feeding people. It's as if she still lives amidst her large joint family back in India.

Bob forces his droopy eyelids open.

"I am as stuffed as a Christmas turkey."

Priya grins at him.

"Ice-cream won't take up space. It will melt into your insides!"

Bob snorts.

"And add inches to my already expanding middle!"

Priya laughs before she shoots back.

"And that's my cue to tell you how fit you are, Mr Bradlee!"

She places the tray on the coffee table before dropping down on the couch next to him.

Bob grimaces.

"The weighing scale is unfortunately not as kind as you, milady."

Priya gives him a friendly poke.

"Enough already!"

Bob eyes the bowl of ice-cream balefully. She had to get his favourite flavour too! He finally gives up and digs in with relish.

The Presidential address draws to a close. Priya picks up the remote and starts surfing channels. Bob catches a glimpse of a familiar face on the screen.

"Hey, wait a minute. I want to see that!"

It is an interview with Prasad Kamineni, the brain behind one of India's leading banks for the poor.

"This was the guy featured in *Newsline*, right?"

Priya's gaze is stuck to the TV as she nods.

Prasad's company, SAMMAAN Microfinance, lends to the poor without any collaterals. A concept that has increasingly caught the eye of the western world, it appears a dignified way of lifting people out of poverty since it offers financial support even to those people who would otherwise be deemed not creditworthy because of their lack of assets.

The company had gone public with a huge and incredibly successful stock market launch. Bob recalls the *Newsline* article carrying an image of the man, flanked by a few of his poor female clients, celebrating their listing at the Indian stock exchange.

The anchor asks Prasad how the idea for a stock issue came about. After all, SAMMAAN is part of the microfinance sector that focuses on the financial empowerment of the poor rather than on hefty profit margins and dizzying dividends, a staple of the commercial markets.

4

"East African Microfinance Bank, a Kenyan microfinance firm, had already demonstrated that microfinance is both a viable as also a profitable investment option. In fact, in 2007 their IPO was 16 times oversubscribed!"

The anchor is suitably impressed.

"That is a formidable record indeed...so have you broken it?"

"We were 25 times oversubscribed, actually!" Prasad Kamineni responds with an almost embarrassed smile.

Bob glances at Priya just in time to catch the obvious pride on her face.

"He is *manavalu*...right?"

Priya turns to him in surprise.

"What did you just say?"

Bob is confused now.

"*Manavalu*...did I get it wrong? Doesn't it mean...our people...I mean your people? Isn't the guy from Andhra Pradesh, too, a Telugu just like you?"

"I'm impressed! Where did you pick that up from?" Bob grins at her.

"That's not relevant. So did I get it right?"

"*Sautakka!*"

"What?"

"Cent percent!"

"That's Telugu too?"

"Hindi."

Bob tries hard to suppress a groan. Priya, like many Indians, is fluent in at least three languages—her mother tongue, Telugu, the national language, Hindi, and English, which has been her medium of instruction.

5

Priya is amused by his expression. Her attention reverts to the TV screen.

"This guy, Kamineni, he hails from a very rich and politically influential family...big shots....*peddavalu* as we call them...and he's been a Wall Street raider besides.

"And he chucked it all for a career in poverty relief!"

"Not like he couldn't afford to!"

Bob chuckles.

"He still didn't have to, Priya. Come on, cut the guy some slack!"

Priya shrugs her shoulders. Bob knows she is deeply prejudiced, thanks to her ancestry. Priya's family comes from the landed class and she nurses a deep guilt for their often inhuman and oppressive ways. Priya has memories of her grandfather doling out punishments as the head of the village *panchayat* (council) by tying transgressors to trees and whipping them. She still shivers when she recalls the cruelty of it. Bob is convinced that it is this guilt that has shaped her convictions and her commitment to grassroots work.

"You have to give it to the man—his company's achievement is remarkable, particularly at a time when the global economy is still in the dumps. And with the market being as volatile as it is!"

Priya's expression turns sober.

"That is so true. I mean millionaires are turning paupers overnight. Remember the instance of Rajaram, the millionaire NRI from LA, who gunned down his entire family before killing himself, after losing all his investments overnight?"

"That was a real tragedy. But the idea of killing yourself over money or the lack of it still kind of rankles!"

Priya gives him a wry look.

"You and I can't even begin to imagine what it is like to have nothing, to be in debt right up to the ears and to have your back against the wall!"

Bob holds up his hands.

"I was just saying that suicide is no solution!"

"I know it is not, but sometimes people know no other solution!"

Bob gets off the couch and stretches.

"What say we take a walk? Let's try and burn at least a fraction of those zillion calories!"

CHAPTER 2

Sri looks at her watch nervously. It is a quarter past ten. She swears under her breath. The things she has to deal with as a working mother! She'd been ready to leave for work when little Nandu threw up all over her crisply starched cotton sari. She could hardly blame him, though. The poor child has been suffering from a runny nose and cough for the last two days. Neither Sri nor her husband Kamal could spare the time to take him to a paediatrician. Work is not much fun these days and the stress at home only makes Sri feel like she is in a pressure cooker ready to blow its lid any minute. With a postgraduate diploma in management, Sri works as executive assistant to Prasad Kamineni, Founder Chairman and Promoter of SAMMAAN Microfinance.

"Sri, do you know how Begumpet got its name?"

Sri turns to look at her colleague, Nilesh, in surprise. After four years of working together, she can actually call him a friend. A young man of amiable disposition, Nilesh

8

is the right hand of the company CEO, Venkat Murthy. The two of them wait for the elevator at the office lobby, a deserted space, as is usual for a Sunday.

Sri is no history buff and all she knows of Begumpet is that it is an exclusive neighbourhood in the Andhra Pradesh state capital, Hyderabad. More importantly, it is where their swank new office building is located.

"No clue, Nilesh!"

"Begumpet is named after the daughter of the sixth Nizam, Basheer Ul-Unnisaa Begum, who received it as part of her wedding dowry. She was married to the second Amir of Paigah, the Shumsul Umra Amir e Kabir. Later the entire village of Begumpet was received by Shahzadi Jahandaar un-nisa Begum, also known as HE Lady Vicar-ul-Umra daughter of HH Nawab Afzal ud Dowla Bahadur, the fifth Nizam of Hyderabad, for her *paandaan ka kharcha*."

Sri smiles in amusement.

"You sound like a talking Wikipedia, Nilesh. But why the sudden interest in the history of this place?"

"I was helping my nephew prepare for his school project. These assignments are more a task for the adults in the family than the kids themselves. You know, my nephew happily went off to play cricket while I did all the hard work!"

Nilesh looks so comically affronted that Sri can't help giggling. The ping of the elevator alerts them to its arrival. They enter and the doors close after them.

It is one of those modern elevators where one side is entirely glass. As the elevator rises, it affords them a clear view of the city vista including the busy Begumpet flyover

9

a fair distance away. Sri and Nilesh catch a glimpse of a procession—such a ubiquitous and integral part of India's democratic landscape—making its way down the flyover.

The office building is one of those modern glass-and-steel structures that typically house IT companies. Although the plush appearance befits their status as the country's leading bank for the poor, Sri has her reservations. The building, or rather its dubious history, makes her uncomfortable.

As they get off the elevator on the eighth floor that houses the offices of the board members and the senior management, she decides to voice her doubts.

"I don't know why, Nilesh, but I've been having a sense of foreboding ever since I heard that this building used to house the offices of Vishwa Computers. One day they were market leaders with international standing, and then, overnight, they were reduced to corporate and social ignominy!"

Nilesh gives her a funny look.

"Sri, don't tell me that you believe in all that Vaastu nonsense?"

Sri bristles before snapping at him.

"Don't call it nonsense. It is based on scientific fact!"

"Yeah, sure. Like the moon is made of green cheese!"

Sri glares as Nilesh guffaws.

"Let's see who has the last laugh. You know, the chief actually sits in the same room that was used by Vishwa's head honcho, Bhaskar Reddy."

Nilesh shrugs as he retorts.

"So what are you worried for? An organizational collapse or that the chief will end up behind bars just like Bhaskar Reddy?"

Sri is not pleased, and her expression makes it evident. Not that it deters him from continuing.

"Come on, Sri! Silly superstitions cannot trigger organizational collapse. Only people and policies can!"

He pauses as a thought strikes him.

"But if coincidences spook you, then let me add to the list. One of our company's independent directors, Vijay Reddy, sits exactly where his guru, Prof Venkat Parikala used to while he was an independent director at Vishwa!"

Sri shakes her head,

"That is certainly not comforting. You do know that Prof Parikala, who was the head of Corporate Governance at the famous Jackson University was actually asked to resign from the board of Vishwa? Vijay put in his papers just last week for reasons unknown."

Nilesh is slightly irritated.

"Sri, we've had a historic IPO and are sitting pretty on over a half a billion dollars of cash. We've been crowned the largest micro-lender in the world. And all you can think of is Vaastu and silly coincidences. I mean, what could possibly go wrong now?"

"Don't tempt fate, Nilesh. More importantly, don't tell me you haven't heard the rumblings from the ground?"

Nilesh does not get a chance to respond as Prasad Kamineni walks in just then.

"Good morning guys, is the board room ready?"

"Yes sir, everything is in order."

"Wonderful. So has Venkat Murthy garu come in yet?" Kamineni directs his question at Nilesh—Venkat Murthy is his boss.

11

Just as Nilesh pulls out his phone to call him, the man in question makes a hurried entry. Kamineni waves jauntily at them before walking towards the boardroom. After cursorily acknowledging their presence, Venkat Murthy follows Kamineni.

While both men are in their mid-forties, their personalities are a study in contrast. A slim, well-groomed man dressed in a well-cut kurta pyjama, Kamineni exudes ethnic chic, as opposed to the corporate dressing favoured by Murthy. In keeping with their style of dress, Kamineni is more informal and approachable while Murthy maintains a formal demeanour at all times.

As they are about to walk into the boardroom, Kamineni turns back and calls out to Sri.

"Sri, I may need you to stay late today. Will make sure you get dropped home, of course."

"Thank you, sir," she responds as she exits and shuts the boardroom door behind her.

Kamineni makes a pretence of studying the papers in front of him. He knows, and Venkat probably does too, that he is just buying time. The papers are hardly relevant to the discussion. They are merely props on the stage that Kamineni has set up.

Venkat eyes him warily as he waits for him to initiate conversation. He had been looking forward to a relaxing Sunday at the club before Kamineni's phone call. Working on Sundays is nothing new but something about Kamineni's tone made Murthy just a little edgy. Kamineni's rather affable manner is just a front for his bulldozer personality.

Kamineni looks up from the papers he's been scanning.

"Venkat, I would like you to tender your resignation," he says in a rather matter-of-fact tone.

Venkat is stunned. He feels completely blindsided. Kamineni had never been one to share the limelight and was a known control freak. And yet, given what Venkat had achieved for the company, he never thought he would actually be ousted!

He weighs his words carefully before responding.

"This is a bit of a surprise, Prasad. Before anything else, could I have the privilege of a reason for your request? At the risk of sounding boastful, I have just led this company to a historically successful IPO. I wouldn't be too wrong if I say that I have delivered the goods and more!"

Kamineni raises his eyebrows, looking perplexed.

"Frankly, you being surprised comes as a surprise, Venkat. I thought this had all been agreed upon. After all, when you received that rather fat bonus of ten million rupees in the first quarter, we had agreed that you would relinquish your responsibilities post-IPO. Between you and me, I was actually inclined to overlook that, had we managed to achieve peaceful co-existence. Unfortunately, our management styles are just too different. I would like you to opt out as soon as possible. I think it's in the best interest of the company to do this quickly and amicably."

Venkat is not inclined to give up without a fight.

"Yes, there was an agreement. But given the spectacular

13

success that I made of the IPO, I think there should be some reconsideration. Particularly in the interest of the shareholders, who have invested in the company because of my credentials and experience?"

Prasad has a smirk on his face as he responds.

"Venkat, the shareholders have served their purpose. I don't think we need to bother too much about them or their sentiments from here on."

Venkat can't believe what he is hearing. He'd always known Prasad was ruthless but the extent of his cold-bloodedness surprises him still. "Damn the shareholders! Is that your sentiment now that we have their money?"

"You may interpret it as you choose. The fact of the matter is that the board has lost confidence in you. They find your penchant for rigid banking type systems and processes irksome. I believe I need to take over day-to-day operations now; it is in the best interest of the company."

Venkat feels nauseous. His stomach has been churning and a part of him seems to be observing what is happening from outside his body. He can see that Prasad is not going to waver and suddenly, it doesn't seem worth fighting for. A wave of tiredness washes over him as he capitulates and says, "Okay then, but I need some time. I hope the company will accept that it owes me that, at the very least!"

Prasad pushes back his chair as he stands up.

"I'm giving you a month, Venkat. But any more and I will be forced to...."

"Will you publicly kick me out?"

Prasad shrugs his shoulders.

"I have no propensity for drama, Venkat. I was just

going to say that I will have to ask the board to dismiss you thereafter. Have a good day."

Kamineni turns on his heels and leaves.

Venkat is left feeling as if he has just been run over by a truck. He looks around at the scene of the crime, the boardroom which he has presided over for so long, and takes comfort in the thought that his case is not unique. This is the feeling one has when one realizes it's all meaningless, the rat race, the struggle for power, the ultimate loss of power, the feeling of being redundant. It is a play that has been enacted before, only this is the first time he is the character being eliminated. An inevitable reversal of roles.

—◦◦◦—

The security guard does not stand a chance against the irate mob. He is just one man against the strength of a hundred plus. And all he has to defend himself with is a baton. He quietly moves out of their way without even token protest. The incensed crowd moves into the office lobby and deposits the pallet it has been carrying on the floor.

Nilesh, who comes running down the stairs on hearing the commotion, is horrified to see the corpse of a middle-aged woman. Her face seems strangely familiar.

"Where is Annayya Garu?"

One of the men, clearly in an inebriated state, shouts at Nilesh.

"Why have you brought this corpse here? Who is she?" Nilesh stutters in response.

"One of Annayya Garu's sisters!"

CHAPTER 3

If purchasing power is any indicator of economic health, then the crowds thronging Manhattan's Fifth Avenue certainly do not indicate a limping global economy. It is the world's most expensive retail address and looks every bit its worth.

Bob and Priya amble along the street, lulled by the balmy weather and the heavy meal they have just consumed. Unlike her shopaholic friends, Priya loves to stroll around in one of the numerous parks or spend time pottering around any of the various museums, whenever she has time off. They walk past Bijan, the men's clothing boutique where a doorman ensures entry only for those who have an appointment and can afford the $1,500 price tag for the dress shirts.

"Our investors range from formal financial institutions, the commercial market, right down to the poor woman in the village who raises cows."

Snatches of the TV interview echo in Bob's mind where the germ of a story idea has firmly implanted itself. He is already composing the brief he needs to shoot off to his

16

editor. So caught up is he in his thoughts that he does not even hear the gruff voice calling out to him.

Priya suddenly clutches his arm, breaking his train of thought. She is not given to public displays of affection and hates even holding hands—a possible fallout of life in a patriarchal society where she was constantly chaperoned and on display. She hates drawing attention to herself.

He looks at her in surprise and then in the direction she points towards.

A nattily dressed, black-haired Indian man in his mid-thirties waves enthusiastically at Bob from across the street. He smiles broadly as he waves back in return.

"That's Mayank Sharma, an acquaintance who works with James Jordin," Bob says to Priya as he watches Mayank walk briskly towards them. His opening volleys always remind Bob of staccato gunshots. No wonder people in the west call Indian English "machine gun English".

"Hey Bob, haven't seen you around in a while! How have you been?"

Mayank shakes Bob's hand enthusiastically, looking curiously at Priya from the corner of his eye. Every time an Indian man meets an Indian woman with a white male, there's always an unhealthy need to define the relationship and establish boundaries. Sometimes, Priya wonders if she really is living in twenty-first-century America.

"I'm good, Mayank. Hope you've been well too. Meet Priya Jothi, a friend and Fulbright scholar at Columbia."

Mayank looks impressed.

"Good to meet you, Priya. Bob may have mentioned, I am a senior consultant with a company called James Jordin."

Priya's polite smile leaves him unprepared for her smart-aleck response.

"Who doesn't know James Jordin, Mayank? You finance guys are constantly in the news these days for your role in triggering off the global economic collapse."

Although taken aback by her directness, Mayank does not let it show.

"Touché!"

He smiles at her before turning to Bob.

"Would you guys like to join me for coffee? Unless, of course, you have other plans..."

Bob shrugs.

"Not particularly. We were just out for a leisurely stroll. Coffee sounds good, as long as you promise not to mix arsenic in it!"

Mayank is surprised.

"And why would I do that?"

"Well, that was not exactly a flattering reference that I made to James Jordin in my last report!"

Mayank gives a shout of laughter.

"It's my day off. So you have nothing to worry about."

Bob turns to Priya.

"I hope you are up for coffee, Priya?"

"Would it be okay if I joined you guys in some time? I have a book I need to pick up."

"Sure thing. We'll be down at Café Sta."

Priya nods before hurrying away towards the bookstore across the street.

18

The waiter has a pencil poised over his pad, ready to scribble down their order.

Bob quickly settles for a cappuccino but Mayank takes his time picking from the variety of exotic items listed on the menu.

"I am sure you crack deals quicker than this!"

Mayank's eyes twinkle.

"That's just my day job."

Bob chuckles and goes back to drafting the note to his editor on his tablet.

"I'll have a Mocha Java, thank you."

The waiter nods his approval, making a note of his choice before he moves away.

"So what next, Bob?" "Mulling over a few ideas. You tell me, what's brewing on Wall Street?"

Mayank gives him a dour look.

"Look elsewhere for your next scoop!"

Bob responds with a broad grin.

Mayank takes a peek at the menu again.

"Fancy splitting an apple pie?"

"No way. After an incredibly heavy lunch, Priya tempted me with my favourite butterscotch ice-cream for dessert."

Mayank looks at Bob speculatively. Bob can almost hear the wheels in his head turning. He is not inclined to offer him any explanation though.

"Come on now, Mayank. You can surely give me some dope without going into specifics!"

Mayank shrugs.

"I've been travelling extensively for the last month or two. Hardly had my ears to the ground."

"Where did you go?"

"All over, actually. I've been handling the emerging markets division."

"That sounds interesting. I assume you are talking about emerging investment opportunities. You should know all about the microfinance rage then?"

Mayank's eyebrows shoot up.

"Tell me the truth. Was your question a coincidence or are you following up on a lead?"

Bob is curious now.

"What lead? I was just watching an interview with this chap, Prasad Kamineni on one of the networks. You must know of the guy, he was even featured in *Newsline.*"

Mayank looks at Bob wryly.

"Of course I do. But, more interestingly, I was part of the James Jordin team that put together a status paper on the microfinance sector."

Bob shakes his head. "Shit man! Is this providence or what? Mayank, can you share that paper with me?"

Mayank nods. "I guess I can. I mean it is not classified information or anything."

Just then, Priya walks towards their table, carrying a bag containing at least a half a dozen books. Bob promptly gets up and pulls her a chair.

"Kid-in-a-candy-shop syndrome?"

Bob smiles warmly as Priya gratefully drops down on to the chair.

"Yeah well, there was a sale!"

Mayank nods in understanding.

"No true blood Indian would miss out on a sale."

"Or American or French or English for that matter. Buying cheap is encoded in our collective DNA!"

Mayank guffaws at Priya's observation.

"What will you have, Priya?"

Priya shakes her head. "Nothing, thanks. The bookstore is run by a friend. We just had a cup of tea together. Are you guys done catching up?"

Bob grins.

"Priya, Mayank met your *manavalu* last month!"

Mayank looks at Bob.

"What was that?"

"Oh that's just Bob's way of showing off his Telugu. I presume he is referring to someone from Andhra. Prasad Kamineni would be my guess."

Mayank nods at Priya.

"Yes he is. So you're from Andhra Pradesh too?"

Priya nods. Mayank turns to Bob.

"That is where much of the action is!"

Priya's gaze shifts from Mayank to Bob.

"What action?"

"We were talking about the microfinance sector. They've gotten Wall Street excited and that is something."

Priya looks at Mayank.

"Significant Wall Street investment in there?"

"Does a billion dollars in the last three years qualify as significant?"

Bob lets out a low whistle.

"So, has there been an exponential growth or is this a sudden spike that we are talking about?"

"Definitely a spike. Till three years ago, the global market investment in microfinance stood at around 30 million dollars."

"And India is the preferred destination?"

"Once again, I leave it to you to interpret the figures. In the last three-year period, global microfinance investment in India was around 860 million."

"Very impressive! Correct me if I am wrong, but this is an industry that primarily serves the poor and the marginalized who have limited access to formal financial services. Why is Wall Street so fascinated with India's poor?"

Priya's smile barely hides the sharpness of her words.

"Wall Street obviously concerns itself with numbers, Priya. And India has half a billion poor who are in need of every kind of financial service, making it the world's largest captive market."

Bob nods at Mayank's response.

"Makes sense. But what makes it even more intriguing is the boom period that you are referring to. I mean this more or less corresponds with the global economic crisis!"

"True. In fact our paper highlights April 2007 as a watershed, for that is when the first lot of social equity investors started getting interested in microfinance, and in India to be specific. Of course the commercial investors soon followed. The growth has been so significant that specialists have actually described microfinance as the preferred subsector within the financial sector for investment bankers."

Priya shakes her head in amazement.

"I'm really intrigued now. I am no economist but I've read enough to know that equity investments in other sectors were less than encouraging during the years of the global financial crisis. Is it the huge numbers of poor alone that make it attractive?"

"Well, I wouldn't discount the fact that Indian microfinance institutions offered better commercial returns than their peers in all other industries and also in all other countries."

Bob makes a quick mental note to append that to his pitch. That should be enough to convince his editor!

CHAPTER 4

Mylaram Kallava is tired of fighting.

She has been fighting for longer than she can remember.

As she waits outside the maternity ward of the Gandhipura town hospital, she desperately prays for good fortune—something she hasn't had in more than three decades!

Her father was one of the victims of a hooch tragedy that had claimed her village when Mylaram was hardly ten. She is the third of her mother's six children. The last one was born after her father's death and had been scorned by her family and villagers alike for having claimed her father's life even before her birth. Mylaram could not, for the life of her, make the connection, but then who cared! As if fearing lifelong scorn, the little girl had allowed pneumonia to consume her when she was hardly four.

Mylaram's mother had almost died giving birth to her last child. She never recovered enough to work thereafter.

24

The responsibility of the family fell on her maternal uncle, who had a family and children of his own.

Mylaram would always remember the large measures of abuse that her aunt served her and her siblings, along with the meagre quantity of food. The lady could hardly be blamed, when she was expected to stretch food barely enough for four to fill more than a dozen stomachs. Education was a luxury simply out of their reach. Mylaram's brothers were sent off to work as agricultural labourers when they were hardly fourteen and twelve.

When Mylaram was sixteen, she fell in love with a man from a neighbouring village. That he was already married and an alcoholic hardly seemed to matter. To Mylaram, he represented an escape from the beggarly existence they led at their uncle's home. She eloped with Balaiah and exchanged garlands with him at a nearby temple.

Once the initial euphoria faded, Mylaram discovered that her husband was a lazy good-for-nothing who viewed her as nothing more than a source of income. He lorded over both his wives, affording them equal time to pay obeisance to him.

Mylaram's family pretty much washed their hands off her, post her elopement. She worked as an agricultural labourer to support herself and her husband—whenever he deigned to spend time with her. But things changed with the birth of her second child. While her first pregnancy had been fairly easy and she had continued to work almost right up to the hour, things changed drastically with the second. There was hardly any interval between the two pregnancies. Worse still, lack of nourishment and proper prenatal care resulted in Mylaram becoming severely anaemic. The doctors at the government health centre told her it was a miracle that the mother and baby had survived. They compelled her to undergo family planning surgery since another pregnancy would most certainly prove fatal. Mylaram was deeply upset since she feared that it would make her husband find himself another woman. She learnt after a few months that he had, in fact, had a third woman tucked away for more than a year!

Mylaram's ill-health made it impossible for her to perform arduous physical labour. With no education and no special skills to earn a living, she took to selling peanuts and other snacks at the bus terminal five kilometres away from her home. She would walk the distance and back, until she managed to buy a second-hand bicycle from her neighbour. Desperate to give her two daughters the benefit of the education she'd never had, Mylaram enrolled them in an English-medium school on the outskirts of her village. Her earnings were barely enough to meet these expenses but Mylaram did not let that discourage her. She borrowed heavily from neighbours and informal moneylenders in the hope that her daughters would eventually find good jobs and help her settle all the debts.

Mylaram was convinced that her luck had turned with the arrival of Ramulamma. The lady was related to the village *panchayat* president. She had acquired an almost goddess-like status in the eyes of the poor village women, when she told them that she worked for DevEx, an organization that was committed to wiping out their sufferings and exploitation at the hands of informal moneylenders or *sahukars*. Most of the villagers were illiterate and had no means of understanding the accounting methods of the *sahukars*. All they knew was that they seemed to be making payments all their lives and yet the principal loan amount hardly diminished. They would be told that those payments were hardly enough to meet the interest. Ramulamma told them that the moneylenders charged them exorbitant and usurious rates of interest that were prohibited under law. The organization she represented had been formed for the primary purpose of reaching out to poor rural folk and meeting their credit and other financial needs. They were going to help them with credit, train them to set up business enterprises and help them save. In short, there was an implicit promise of a golden future. Mylaram was among the first batch of women to join the organization and avail of their credit facilities. Her first loan went towards buying a pushcart that would help her transport her wares to the bus terminal and back. She took a second loan to set up a small mobile eatery. She was immensely gratified by the response to the eatery and the resultant spurt in income. She was now emboldened to take a loan to gift somewhat high-end phones to her daughters. The two girls had not had an easy life and Mylaram did not want their youth to be as harsh and barren as hers had been.

While Mylaram dreamt of her daughters getting a good education and well-paying jobs, her older daughter decided to take a leaf out of her book. She fell in love with a man who was as much of a good-for-nothing as her father. Thankfully, he was not already married. But his reputation, as well as the fact that he belonged to a different caste, did not exactly endear him to Mylaram. Faced with stiff opposition, her daughter, like her, eloped with her lover.

After much screaming and chest-beating, Mylaram had taken her daughter back a year later, when she was three months pregnant and her husband had taken off for parts unknown. Much as she resented the girl for her actions, she could hardly abandon her to fate. Besides, Mylaram desperately needed a helping hand at home.

Her second daughter had been falling ill once too often. She was unable to attend classes regularly and could not help with the business either. Visits to the village primary health centre and even the local tantric had not yielded any results. The girl continued to suffer from acute abdominal pain.

Mylaram now had to divide her time between her business and ferrying her younger daughter around to various hospitals. Finally, the girl was diagnosed with an infected appendix and advised surgery. The nearest government hospital was more than seventy kilometres away. This forced Mylaram to take her daughter to a private hospital closer to home. Faced with huge medical expenses, Mylaram was grateful when Ramulamma recommended her case and got her an emergency loan to cover them.

The surgery was successful and Mylaram was able to bring her daughter home a week later. The girl was weak and ill and needed constant care. Mylaram's older daughter was a huge support. It was the monsoon season and Mylaram had to contend with a leaking roof. She already had two loans running concurrently with DevEx.

It was then that Ramulamma introduced her and the other women to Sarasakka, a representative of another organization like hers called SAMMAAN Microfinance. They were kind enough to lend Mylaram money to cover the medical expenses and then gave her a second loan for house repairs. While Mylaram was grateful for all the money she got, she was now struggling to repay the instalments every month. And while they had been very kind to begin with, the organizational representatives, including Ramulakka, were now beginning to talk tough. Since the loans were issued on a group guarantee basis, she was also under severe pressure from her peers. She was behind her repayment schedule by more than three months and was now desperately hoping for some good fortune to help her repay the loans.

Despite Mylaram's hopes, ill luck had refused to leave her side. One day her older daughter complained of acute abdominal pain. Fearing complications in her pregnancy, the local midwife advised Mylaram to take her to the town hospital.

It is outside the maternity ward of that very hospital that Mylaram now waits. Scared, she continues to pray for good news.

A nurse exits the ward and calls out to her.

Mylaram rushes to her side and looks at her fearfully.

"Your daughter has survived but the baby is lost. The foetus was not properly formed, though. You can take your daughter home the day after."

The nurse turns on her heel and goes back in, leaving Mylaram unsure of what to feel. Is she supposed to celebrate her daughter being alive, grieve over the lost child or be grateful that it did not survive to live a deformed life?

The nurse returns with a chit in hand.

"You need to pay Rs 5,000 before we can discharge your daughter."

Mylaram is stunned. She had not thought of this part at all. While she was already hard-pressed for money to meet loan repayments, here was an additional expense!

A tired Mylaram takes a bus back home in the evening. As she walks forlornly towards her hut, she is stopped in her tracks by a few women, who are her fellow group[1] members.

"What happened to Kala?" asks one of the women.

"She survived but the baby is gone," answers Mylaram, mournfully.

"That is sad. But maybe it is better not to have the offspring of a son of a bitch who has dumped her this way!" observes another woman.

"How can we hold the father's crimes against the child? She is devastated for the child was still her flesh and blood!"

Mylaram starts to walk away when one of the women holds her by the arm.

"The loan recovery agents will be here the day after."

Mylaram looks tired and defeated.

"I don't have the money to repay them."

"You can't do that! My daughter's wedding will be ruined then!"

---

1 A Joint Liability Group (JLG) typically consists of five to ten women who are lent money under a microfinance initiative.

Mylaram looks at her in alarm.

"What are you saying?"

"Mylaram, you know the loan terms as well as we do. One of us defaults on her repayment and all of us suffer!"

Mylaram feels her head begin to spin.

"If my loan does not come through, my daughter's wedding will be stalled. We will be shamed before the whole world and will have no other option but to kill ourselves. And our deaths will be on you!"

The woman speaks in a tone that is a mix of a curse and a plea.

Mylaram does not know what to say. She nods her head slowly and walks back home.

Her younger daughter is waiting.

"Mother, is Akka alright?"

Mylaram nods her head before curling up in a corner. She cannot cope with questions.

The next day she collects whatever little cash she has, puts together anything of value in the house and takes it to the scrap shop in town.

She begs and pleads with the scrap dealer to give her a good deal. Lady luck finally shines on her, or maybe the scrap dealer is just in a charitable mood. Mylaram gets enough to meet the hospital expenses and some more.

She goes to the hospital, gets her daughter discharged and brings her back home.

That night, she cooks a good meal and feeds her daughters with her own hands. Then, she goes to sleep, hugging them both.

The next morning, the loan recovery agents from DevEx arrive in the village.

They are just in time to see her hanging from the very roof that they had lent her money to repair.

CHAPTER 5

NEW YORK, 20 SEPTEMBER 2010

"The number you are calling is either switched off or cannot be reached at the moment."

Bob swears loudly. He has been getting the same response over the last couple of days. Where the hell *is* Chandresh ?

Chandresh had been the first person Bob had called after the editor gave his nod for the story. A former special correspondent with one of India's leading national dailies, Chandresh specialized in offbeat development stories. Bob had first made his acquaintance while working on a report on the phenomenon of farmer suicides in India. One of his classmates from Columbia, a scion of one of India's leading publishing families, had introduced him to Chandresh. The two had kept in touch ever since, sharing stories and gossip that came to their notice and which they thought might be relevant to the other.

Just then, Bob's phone rings and he picks it up eagerly, hoping it is Chandresh.

The call is from Mayank Sharma. Bob's irritation fades when he hears his voice.

"Hey Mayank, what's up man?"

"Hi Bob, all set to fly out to India?"

"Yeah, working on last minute details. Was just trying to reach a local contact."

"Hope the paper I forwarded to you was useful!"

"It really was, Mayank. Helped me put together a basic framework for the article."

"Glad I could help. I have some more good news for you. Prasad Kamineni is addressing a gathering at the Cramer Institute for Research on Inclusive Growth (CIRIG) in Boston on Friday. I have an invite for you, in case you'd like to go."

"Mayank, I owe you big on this one! I'll see you there on Friday."

"Will make sure to collect when James Jordin needs a puff piece!"

Mayank laughs before hanging up.

The apartment door opens and Priya enters. Her sharp eye spots the look of contained excitement on Bob's face.

"Got through to Chandresh?"

"Not yet. But I am going to meeting your *manavalu* on Friday!"

—◌◌◌—

The cabbie who drives Bob from the Boston airport to the CIRIG office in the central business district turns out to be Indian. A turbaned gentleman, he introduces himself as Sardar Kanwal Singh. The man is quite garrulous for so early in the day.

"I am from Punjab," he announces rather proudly, before quickly clarifying that it is the one in India. "Did you know there is a Punjab in Pakistan too?"

Bob nods and tells him he has read a lot on Indian history.

"Then you must know about the Partition?"

"Yes, I do."

"My father lost his parents and brothers on a train, while they were trying to flee Pakistan."

"I am really sorry to hear that."

"My father's brother was a baby. Three months old! Heartless bastards."

Bob sighs and nods in commiseration.

"Terrible what happened to the twin towers."

Bob senses the direction in which the conversation is going.

"How much longer before we get there?"

"Sir, please take a look at the GPS. I am following the correct route with the least traffic. It won't take much longer. I am a very honest man. I would not bring disrepute to my country in a foreign land."

Bob assures the man that he does not doubt his integrity.

"So, what do you do?"

"What do you think?"

"A banker?"

The man's tone reveals that he does not look at bankers favourably. Pretty much in sync with the national sentiment, Bob thinks to himself as he chuckles.

"No, I am a journalist."

Sardar Kanwal Singh is intrigued.

"Digging for a scam?"

"For a change, I am going to report on the rich who are investing to improve the lives of the poor!"

The man has no comeback for that.

———

With hardly a week left before his departure to India, the trip to Boston had been a bit of a squeeze, but Bob was not going to pass on an opportunity to hobnob with some of the biggest names in inclusive finance, all gathered under one roof.

On entering the hall, the guests are handed out booklets on SAMMAAN Microfinance Limited, which include a brief write-up on the founder, Prasad Kamineni. Bob idly leafs through one as he waits for the event to begin.

SAMMAAN Microfinance empowers the poor to become economically self-reliant by providing financial services in a sustainable manner. Launched in 1994, SAMMAAN Microfinance is one of the fastest growing microfinance institutions in the world, having provided over $800 million (INR 3,200 crore) as loans and has maintained loans outstanding of $423 million (INR 1,692 crore) to over 2 million women members in the poorest regions of India. Borrowers take loans for income-generating activities including livestock rearing, agriculture, trade (fruit/vegetable vending), production (basket and carpet weaving, pottery) and businesses like spas, beauty parlours, game parlours and photography. SAMMAAN also offers very low interest loans for emergencies and life and health insurance to its members. Its NGO wing, SAMMAAN Foundation, runs the Pro-Poor Programme.

SAMMAAN currently has 900 microfinance branches in 19 states across India, and aims to reach 7,000,000 members by end of 2010. In the last year alone, SAMMAAN Microfinance has achieved nearly 392% growth, with 99.98% on-time repayment rate.

The founder of SAMMAAN, Prasad Kamineni, has dedicated much of his professional life to addressing India's development and growth, right from the grass-roots. Prior to launching SAMMAAN, Prasad worked on a research project on gender, microfinance and family dynamics in India, Bangladesh and Nepal. He has also worked as a field level supervisor with Madhya Bharath Vikas Sanstha, an NGO working in the area of rural enterprise development. He has written extensively in world class publications including the *Cramer Economic Review*. He holds a BA in Economics from St Stephen's College, New Delhi, an MA in Development Economics from Oxford and a PhD from the University of Michigan, where his dissertation focused on bottom of the pyramid strategies. He also has experience working in the formal financial sector in his brief career with Grantham FinCorp, a leading investment firm on Wall Street.

A round of polite applause alerts Bob to the arrival of the guests of honour. Kamineni is flanked by the director of CIRIG and other senior officials.

A CIRIG official called Che makes introductory remarks on the stated mission of the institution: CIRIG partners with multi-lateral and bi-lateral agencies, private foundations, and national governments that share a common vision of improving the lives of poor people with better access to finance and related services.

Bob alternates between doodling idly and making quick notes on important observations. He hopes to corral Kamineni for a one-on-one later.

Some of the statistics that Che's presentation throws up underline the appalling state of affairs where an estimated 3.1 billion working-age adults—more than half of the world's total adult population—have no access to any kind of formal financial services that the privileged consider a basic necessity. No banks with which to deposit savings or access loans, no credit cards to swipe without a second thought, for necessary purchases or an impulse buy. Their livestock and pieces of jewellery are their means to save and pawn brokers their only source of credit, no matter how high the risk or how low the returns. Welfare measures and philanthropic initiatives have thus formed the mainstay of efforts to service the financial needs of the poor to a degree.

Che touts the emergence of microfinance as that miracle solution that has successfully dispelled the notion that the poor are a risky investment, by ensuring their access to financial services and more importantly, attracting commercial capital as investment into the sector.

There is polite applause all around as Che goes on to cite the stupendous success of the SAMMAAN IPO. A beaming Kamineni is thereafter invited to offer his insights on the evolution of the Indian microfinance sector from a subsidy dependent, pro-poor initiative to a commercially viable enterprise that is still sensitive to the needs of its target clientele.

Kamineni turns out to be a witty speaker and quite adept at keeping an audience engaged. Bob cannot help but be impressed by the combination of sincerity and confidence in his demeanour.

"The degree of financial exclusion faced by the poor in India, where almost 80 percent of its 1.2 billion population live on less than US$2 per day, is simply phenomenal. This scenario makes it, by many estimates, the largest potential microfinance market in the world.

While in all fairness, right from the nineteenth century onwards, India has initiated several progressive financial inclusion efforts ranging from the postal savings banks to cooperative financial institutions, regional rural banks etc., none of these have been successful."

He pauses and looks enquiringly at his audience.

"Anyone know why?"

There is silence in the room.

"These initiatives were regularly written off as bad debts. I am sure all of you recall the Rs 95,000-crore loan waiver for farmers before the general elections of 2009. Loans have essentially been doled out through melas[2] and are typically

---

2 Melas are socio-economic congregations, where all and sundry get loans en-masse usually without any serious analysis by the lenders of their clients' ability to service their debt.

based on contacts, influence and bribery. As a result, more often than not, the recovery rate is extremely low."

As Kamineni pauses to take a sip of water, Bob marvels at his well-timed and strategic pause. The silence will serve to underline the next point he intends to make. Kamineni's words confirm this.

"The success achieved by microfinance institutions like SAMMAAN becomes even more phenomenal in the light of all this. This shift from being a charitable trust to a non-banking finance company has enabled SAMMAN to raise more capital and grow much faster. Today, NBFC microfinance institutions account for more than four-fifths of all MFI loans, dominated by the five largest MFIs, including SAMMAAN. That international investment firms and financial institutions are eager to partner with us is proof of the degree of success the sector has achieved in terms of sheer numbers, be it outreach or profits."

He pauses yet again before reeling off names of some of the key investors in the Indian microfinance sector. Bob is amazed to hear mention of "Greek billionaire Alexander Zaimis and the Indian IT moghul, Raghava Shetty".

"We had a phenomenally successful IPO where $680 million was raised as fresh capital. In fact, post the IPO, SAMMAN's valuation stood at $4.8 billion with an almost 84% rise in the share price after nearly four weeks of trading. SAMMAAN has been among the fastest growing microfinance institutions globally, with a compound annual growth rate of 262% since 2004. More importantly, the SAMMAAN IPO has demonstrated that microfinance institutions can successfully harness the vast resources of capital markets. And that's a potentially game-changing development. Thank you ladies and gentlemen."

During the resounding applause that follows, Bob cannot help but wonder at the almost fairy tale-like quality of the SAMMAAN success story. The figures that Kamineni has bandied about are all fine and dandy, but the ultimate proof lies in the degree of success achieved with regard to the larger goal of inclusion and the difference it has made to the lives of the clientele. Something that Bob plans to verify once he gets to the field.

Bob's scepticism seems to find resonance in the observations made by a few other panelists. David Harding, a fellow at the Institute of Afro-Asian Development Studies at Reading, UK, and Prof Raman, a senior Indian academician engaged in development research, both express huge reservations about the actual benefits for the poor as well as the not-so-ethical tactics adopted by the institutions in the process of their evolution to for-profit forms.

"There have been challenges, owing to legal restrictions, in the transference of funds from a non-profit NGO to a private limited company. Spurred on by the need for growth, most MFIs have resorted to the creation of illegal mutual benefit trusts through which to channelize resources including external capital. Since incorporation as an NBFC requires a minimum capital requirement of Rs 2 crore, some of the MFIs have even stooped as low as to transfer the compulsory savings of their NGO clients to the MBTs and thereafter the NBFC. They've been further assisted by transformation loans offered by state-owned development banks to NGOs at phenomenally low rates of interest.

There have also been instances of other institutions raising the conversion capital required through donor grants to the NGO, which have been subsequently routed to the MFIs. In all of these cases, the clients have been issued shares in the MBT, which in turn invested in the MFI's shares."

Prof Raman speaks in a measured tone as he meticulously exposes strategies used by MFIs that are both legally and ethically unsound. Despite his dispassionate tone, his disillusionment and anger come through clearly in his words.

"It was in the years following 2006 that foreign funds started flowing heavily into the MFIs, allowing further expansion of operations and the size of client portfolios. Consequent to the profit margins achieved by the MFIs, the value of their scrips skyrocketed in the market. However, the poor women clients, who had borne the risk of the business originally by way of investing their savings in the NGO, did not benefit in the least from this success story.

The shares owned by the women had been transferred back to the original promoters or employees of the MFI within a few years of their issuance at a far lower price. Compare that to the killing that the promoters and MFI employees subsequently made by selling the shares to the venture capitalists, investment firms, etc. These are some of the negative aspects of commercialization, and I rest my case."

Bob is so busy making frantic notes that he doesn't observe Kamineni's reaction to Prof Raman's observations. However, as the latter walks past Prasad Kamineni to resume his seat after the presentation, Bob notices Kamineni's body language stiffen, even as he courteously nods at the professor.

"At the risk of sounding a bit crass, Wall Street's interest in the microfinance sector seems to me a bit like a butcher investing in animal shelters."

Wall Street observer Tom Moody has the audience tittering with his opening remark. Kamineni and other CIRIG officials are not amused.

In an attempt at striking a conciliatory note, Moody clarifies that, given the huge numbers of poor people in India, the sector offers a hugely viable and secure investment opportunity to the capital markets, particularly in the face of the global economic crisis.

"The microfinance sector, particularly in India, can even be called the sunrise industry. The global economic crisis had investors scrambling to uncover new, emerging opportunities that offered high returns on investment, besides. Given its spectacular showing, the microfinance sector presented itself as that opportunity. The poor seemed to be the most bank-worthy and proved to be a somewhat safe and secure investment alternative. India scored primarily because globally, it had the largest captive market of the poor. The spectacular success achieved by the East African Microfinance Bank IPO in Kenya in the months just preceding the crisis may have also encouraged investors who believed that this was a route that the Indian microfinance sector could well take in the years to come."

Flashing a half apologetic smile at Kamineni, he adds,

"While SAMMAAN's hugely successful IPO seems to lend credence to Wall Street's belief, a careful analysis appears to indicate that the numbers just don't add up and are out of sync with market peers. Stated differently, while the earning prospects at SAMMAAN are indeed attractive, I am not sure that they justify such a high valuation."

Bob is watching Kamineni intently now, but the latter remains impassive right through Moody's speech.

When Vincent Bell, a senior analyst with Enterprise Global, which has invested heavily in Indian microfinance, describes the inflow of commercial capital into the sector as a heaven-sent opportunity, Bob has a sudden mental image of Wall Street knights, dressed in flowing capes and astride white steeds, riding hard to bail out a sector in distress.... Blame it on a reporter's natural cynicism!

James Henderson, a former central banker, remarks that policy makers all over the world are recognizing that financial exclusion is a risk to political stability.

"The financial sector is similar to a three-legged stool, where, if the law is the seat, regulations are the legs. One leg is safety and soundness, another is profitability and innovation, and the third is consumer protection. Each leg is equally strong and essential to maintaining balance. It is through effective and balanced regulations and rules that the system has retained its integrity, its edge and its ability to deliver capital where it is needed. The general consensus is that regulations should allow this more risky activity to be profitable. In that context, even countries like Brazil, Kenya, the Philippines and several others are light years ahead of India"

'REGULATORY FRAMEWORK?'

Bob scribbles these words down before thickly

underlining them. What about it? How much had it benefited Kamineni in achieving the numbers that he had? Bob mentally shakes himself as he realizes that he is already allowing himself to be influenced and forming opinions before even getting started.

"He may not be a knight in shining armour but there is no reason to conclude that he is a bluebeard!" he tells himself.

As the proceedings draw to a close, Bob walks up to Kamineni, who is already surrounded by a group of people who want more of his time and attention. Kamineni does not seem inclined to linger and excuses himself, saying he has a flight back home later in the evening. Unwilling to let go of the opportunity of an introduction, Bob presses his way forward and hands his business card to Kamineni. The name of the publication he represents does the trick, like always. Kamineni offers Bob an ingratiatingly charming smile as he pleads his inability to offer him time immediately.

Bob nods in understanding.

"Not a problem at all, Mr Kamineni. You'll be pleased to know that I will be in India in a few days' time. We are working on a story on the stupendous growth of the Indian microfinance sector and, in particular, the investments flowing in from the capital markets. Obviously, the success story of your IPO will figure prominently in the article. I would be most grateful if you can spare time for me in India. And maybe introduce me to your clientele, particularly those women who got a taste of corporate India when they accompanied you to the Bombay stock exchange!"

"That is wonderful news. We would be delighted to have

you over at SAMMAAN. Look forward to meeting you in India then."

He thrusts his own business card into Bob's hands.

"This card has my direct number. Call me as soon as you get to Hyderabad and we will be happy to offer you our hospitality."

Bob thanks him and the two men shake hands before Kamineni leaves, accompanied by CIRIG officials.

As he looks around the room, Bob notices Tom Moody and Prof Raman deep in conversation with a small group of others. Dissonant voices always add colour and strength to a story. As Bob approaches the duo, he can't help but feel pleased that his story seems to be taking shape even before he has left American shores.

CHAPTER 6

HYDERABAD, 23 SEPTEMBER 2010

The man is so engrossed in the papers in his folder that he barely notices the commotion outside his car window.

"We need to go to the Principal Secretary's office!"

It is his driver's voice that alerts Rashid to his surroundings. A fairly senior bureaucrat, Rashid looks his part—with his bush shirt and corpulent presence. He is surprised. The government insignia on his car's license plates usually guarantees smooth entry into any official premises.

The policeman tries to peer past the driver to catch a glimpse of Rashid.

"Saab is the CEO of TERP!"

The policeman is clearly puzzled.

"Arre… Trust for Eradication of Rural Poverty. Please don't waste *Saab's* time. He has to go to the CM's house next!"

The mention of the Chief Minister works like magic and the car is allowed to pass through.

"What is happening, Gopal? Why is there such heightened security?"

The driver is surprised. Has his boss not heard the news?

"Sir, there is that procession today against the suicides, *na*! Also, they are threatening to bomb the Secretariat."

Of course, the papers had carried reports. Rashid had been so busy mulling over the upcoming meeting that he had forgotten all about it. The Principal Secretary was a very business like man and did not appreciate his time being wasted. And certainly not at a moment like this.

The Andhra Pradesh Secretariat building is a rather fine piece of architecture, just a few years short of celebrating its centenary. It is the seat of power in the state, both legislative and bureaucratic. A high security zone even on normal days, today it resembles a fortress. There is a whole battalion of security personnel milling all over the place, doing a thorough check of anyone who attempts to enter the premises.

Rashid jumps out of the car even as it slows down before Sampreethi, the Secretariat's L block, and dashes into the building, hurriedly flashing his ID at the security personnel who try to stop him. On normal occasions, he would have flexed his bureaucratic muscles a bit. But there is hardly time for that today.

Rashid glances at his watch repeatedly as he makes his way into the Principal Secretary's office, where he is greeted by Subbalakshmi Srinivas, the efficient administrative assistant.

"Does he have someone with him or can I go in?"

She shakes her head.

"He's waiting for you. Please go right in."

He groans inwardly and hurries into the inner chamber.

The Principal Secretary, Maruti Rao, better known as MR, stands by the window, gazing at the large expanse of sun-dappled water that represents the Hussain Sagar Lake. Rashid doubts if he is appreciating the scenic view, though, since a frown mars his forehead. The frown deepens when he sees Rashid enter.

"Sorry, sir. But the traffic jam was terrible. And then all that security! Sir, I believe the traffic has been disrupted in several parts of the city thanks to the procession of anti-MFI protestors. Of course, the intelligence report that Maoists may be mingling with the crowds and trying to bomb the secretariat, sir...."

Rashid comes to a halt as he realizes he is babbling. Maruti Rao looks irritated.

"We need to rush if we are to get to the CM's house in time. No time for a chat. You can update me on our way there."

With that, MR quickly walks out of his room with Rashid almost running behind him to keep pace.

They are soon seated in the car and heading towards the Chief Minister's official bungalow.

"So, what is the latest?"

"There have been reports of four more in the last two days, sir!"

MR frowns.

"Why am I not surprised?"

"Sir, the MFIs are fully to blame. But the Maoists are,

of course, working at the grassroots to rouse popular sentiment against the government on this. There has to be some swift and hard action."

MR sighs before answering.

"We need to have a watertight case that will stand in a court of law."

"Sir, the families of the victims would surely be willing to testify. In the guise of inclusion, they have allowed their greed to prevail and pushed more than fifty people to kill themselves so far!"

"Be careful, Rashid. You head a rival programme and the MFI lobby will only accuse you of misrepresenting facts."

"Sir, the SHG model of microcredit has been in existence for over two decades. And we have no personal or vested interest in any case."

"That is not how they will see it. They will come up with their own line of argument in any case, including how the government is trying to crush free enterprise to further its own obsolete programmes."

The CM's bungalow, a beautiful white building on Raj Bhavan Road, comes into sight and this puts an end to the discussion.

The guards have already been intimated of their visit and they wave the car through.

As the two wait in the anteroom to the CM's office, MR points to the files that Rashid is carrying.

"I hope you are carrying documentary proof of one or two of these MFI-related suicide cases?"

"Yes, sir. There is information on as many as seven of them here."

MR nods as they wait to be summoned in. He hopes the documentary evidence will convince the CM of the need for urgent action.

Rashid starts flipping through his papers like a student outside an examination hall. MR can't help but feel somewhat amused at his junior colleague's obvious nervousness.

Just then, the door opens and the CM's private secretary beckons them to enter.

Rashid jumps, almost dropping the file in a hurry. MR gives him a calming look before walking into the room.

The CM and his cabinet colleague, the Rural Development Minister, are already seated. The officials greet them with the customary deference before gratefully taking their seats.

The CM, a former footballer, is of athletic build. The rural development minister, who belongs to the moneylender community, is prosperously plump.

"How did things turn so bad all of a sudden? Why was the administration at the ground level not alert to the goings on?" asks the CM.

"Sir, it is obviously not an overnight phenomenon. The MFIs' activities have clearly gone unchecked for some time now, thanks to the perception that they are our partners in change."

The CM is perceptibly disturbed.

"I understand that development initiatives need to be able to sustain themselves. But growing at the cost of the very lives that they swore to better?"

MR is only too aware of the CM's way with words. That and his oratory skills have won him both hearts and votes in the last thirty years of his political career.

"True, sir. The situation is quite grim and getting worse as we speak. And of course the Maoist threat is only compounding it."

The CM glances at MR at the mention of the Maoists. He knows of his history with them. MR was among the seven officers kidnapped by Maoists while visiting a village in their stronghold territory where a dam was to be constructed. He had successfully negotiated their freedom, with some help from the government, of course, but was since identified as someone who had some influence with them. In fact, writing a book on the incident was on MR's post-retirement agenda, but that would have to wait for another three years.

"So what are we going to do about them? And I mean the suicides, of course."

MR looks up as the CM shoots the question at him. Nodding his head, he points to Rashid.

"Sir, Rashid will apprise you of the situation first. He has prepared detailed case studies of the seven suicides triggered by the actions of the MFIs. He is ready with a presentation."

Rashid is taken aback. He had thought he would be required to chip in with a few odd statistics here and there. He never expected to have to make a presentation!

"Sir...that is...the situation is very grim, sir."

The CM cuts in rather abruptly.

"I don't think we have time for long stories. Keep it quick and short. We need to be looking at corrective actions."

Rashid is half relieved that he will not be expected to expound at length.

"Sir, nine people have died in Warangal and Ranga Reddy districts due to harassment by MFI agents."

The Rural Development Minister decides to offer an opinion.

"These MFIs are like leeches that bleed people dry. First, they over-lend and then they arm-twist people into repaying the loans at really high rates of interest. They even put my moneylending caste to shame!"

The CM is not particularly impressed by the minister's efforts to seek brownie points for his caste. But when caste and coalitions are what help governments in India stay in power, it is important to ignore irrelevant details.

"Looks like the government and the Maoists are fighting the same evil for a change, eh Marutigaru?"

The CM looks at MR with a half-smile. MR nods, fully aware that the CM is trying to test his allegiance. Who is he to disappoint him?

"Indeed sir! The Maoists have a history of locking horns with informal financiers. That was made amply clear to us all those years ago when they took us captive at Gurtedu. But of course, the onus is now ours."

The CM acknowledges this with a nod before gesturing to Rashid to continue.

"Sir, in almost all the cases, there has been an instance of over and multiple lending, There has been indiscriminate lending and gross violations of all ground-level procedures, sir."

The CM turns to MR.

"I want a report from across the state. Get your teams in

all the districts to file a report on all such instances within their purview within the next 48 hours."

He turns back to Rashid.

"I want TERP to come up with a comprehensive report on the causes of the suicides."

He finally turns to his cabinet colleague to issue another set of directives.

"Consult with the Ministry of Law on the status of the existing laws that apply to MFIs. Get hold of the Memorandum and Articles for some of these MFIs and have our legal experts study them. Talk to the Federal Banking Regulator and see what they advise on treating the MFIs as common moneylenders under these circumstances."

He returns his attention to MR.

"About this threat...have they targeted the MFIs directly? Or are they reserving all their ire for the government?"

"Sir, they have issued a direct threat to them. Here, I have a copy of a newspaper report on it."

SHUT SHOP IN VILLAGES, MAOISTS TELL MFIs

ENN Sep 23, 2010, 03.33am IST

WARANGAL: Taking a tough stand against micro finance institutions (MFIs), the Maoists have asked MFI managements to close their operations in villages immediately in the wake of series of suicides by women.

Maoist party KKW (Karim-nagar-Khammam-Warangal)

Secretary Sudhakar warned MFIs of dire consequences if they do not shut shop. In a statement here on Friday, he said agents and representatives of MFIs are humiliating rural women and insulting their family members because of which several villagers have committed suicide.

He also warned SAM-MAAN Microfinance Chief Prasad Kamineni, owners of DevEx, Asshray and Sowmya, of serious consequences as "they are responsible for the spate of suicides in the state," he said in the statement.

Sudhakar said the government should grant five acres of agricultural land, an ex gratia of Rs 5 lakhs, and employment for one member of the families of the deceased.

Making an appeal to the youth and women associations to fight against the fast-mushrooming MFI branches in the state, he said the government must take necessary steps to cancel the licences of these MFIs. Sudhakar warned MFIs about their anti-people policies. "If you do not change your attitude, we will teach you a fitting lesson," he stated.

Meanwhile, four Maoists have been arrested in Moranchapalle village in Bhupalapalle mandal. They were nabbed from the forest area. Fourteen country-made rifles have been recovered from them.

The CM seems perturbed as he scans the report.

"Have you alerted the police and the home ministry on this? We need to provide the MFIs security whatever be their crimes."

The CM closes his eyes and pinches the bridge of his nose.

"And keep the media at bay until we come up with a plan of action."

CHAPTER 7

PADERU VILLAGE, ANDHRA PRADESH,
24 SEPTEMBER 2010

"It is even being said that some MFI bosses have hired private security guards to protect them from the ire of their clientele. The incident at the offices of SAMMAAN and the subsequent threat by the Maoists has the sector truly shaken up. Once regarded as a gold mine, it is now a hornet's nest that the recent spate of suicides has stirred up. This is Bhagyaraj S. reporting for Zion TV from Warangal."

Chandresh Rajan stubs his cigarette into the chipped coffee cup being used as an ashtray. He picks up the remote lying on the table and cuts the anchor short as she launches into a story on factional fighting in the ruling party. It will be another couple of hours before his escort arrives; for now, the dingy walls of his hotel room seem to be closing in on him. He remembers spotting a small tea shop down the road. The idea of a cup of tea is appealing to him.

As he steps out of the spartan building, he takes a deep breath, filling his lungs with the pristine air of the hills. It feels good to be inhaling something other than diesel fumes and the stench of rotting garbage or human waste. There are hardly half a dozen people on the road, four of them on foot and two on cycles. They eye him suspiciously. Despite his inconspicuous personality, they clearly identify him as an outsider. Strangers are not greeted warmly in these parts. One can hardly blame the locals, though, for such has been their experience.

Paderu, a remote village in the hills of Vizag, a district of coastal Andhra, is Maoist heartland, after all. A part of the Dandakaranya region spreads across Andhra Pradesh, Chhattisgarh and Orissa, and Paderu has a significant tribal population. A significant raison d'être for the Maoist movement is the exploitation of tribal resources by the political class. It is to speak to one of the Maoist leaders that Chandresh is here in Paderu. After years of working for a leading publication in the country, he is now a syndicated columnist focusing on development and grassroots issues.

As Chandresh walks towards the tea shop, his mind goes back to the news report that he just caught on TV. Clearly the issue is erupting and in a big way. What is surprising is that it has taken so long for the can of worms to open. He had written an article almost a year ago indicating that the growth of the sector was more a matter of concern than celebration, since it was happening at the cost of the very clientele it had sworn to serve. In fact, infamy and the sector were no strangers to each other. Less than five years ago, a tussle between two competing MFIs had thrown up a stench so strong that a magisterial enquiry had been ordered. What was happening today was the same in many ways and yet had a whole new dimension to it, in the form of commercial and foreign capital.

Chandresh is so caught up in his thoughts that he ends up walking past the tea shop before realization strikes. He retraces his steps and slumps on a bench outside the tea shop.

"One *chai* please...and make it double strong!"

The shop owner nods as he pumps the kerosene stove hard, to get it to burn better. He does not appear inclined to chat, quite uncommon given that tea shop owners are quite often a great source of village gossip. Like before, Chandresh recognizes this as a peculiarity of the territory they are in. The tea shop owner makes a froth on top that would put a barista from Starbucks to shame, by pouring one cup of tea into another—the further apart he spreads his arms, the better the froth.

The tea arrives, piping hot and with a lovely aroma. Chandresh sighs in appreciation after the first sip. It is so different from the tea you find in tea shops in the city, so much better than the weak tea that he is forced to sip at fancy five-star hotels, while attending seminars and the like.

Chandresh's gaze wanders around, looking for interesting sights the details of which he could incorporate in his column. He spots an old man sitting on a bench placed just a few feet away from the tea shop, quietly sipping his tea and trying to look inconspicuous. However, almost every passerby greets him respectfully, indicating that he is a man of some local repute.

The man's face is deeply tanned and wrinkled, bearing testimony to long years of hard living. His eyes are deep-set and penetrating. He looks up for a moment and catches Chandresh looking at him. He reciprocates with a long measured look of his own. Chandresh, who has met more than his share of intimidating personalities in the course of his career, is not one to be easily disconcerted. Yet, he is the first to avert his eyes, feeling almost guilty for having invaded the man's private space, even while the journalist in him feels compelled to reach out and speak to the man, to know the stories hidden in the depths of those sunken eyes. He pays for the tea and a handful of nuts wrapped in a paper cone, before walking toward the old man.

The bench is placed to the right of the shack that houses the tea shop. Chandresh greets the old man politely before looking ahead at the majestic view that the spot affords. The sky is painted in shades of blue and white and the sun's warmth is a benign grace that offers protection against the nip in the air.

Chandresh rummages through his pockets for his pack of cigarettes when a thought strikes him.

"Could I bum a cigarette off you, please?"

It was a clichéd opening gambit but he couldn't think of anything better.

The old man looks at him in amusement.

"Do I look like a man who smokes the expensive brands that you city folk patronize?"

Chandresh shakes his head hurriedly.

"A *beedi* would do just as well. I am not particular!"

The old man gives him a knowing look before pulling out a *beedi* from a roll tucked away in the upper folds of his faded dhoti.

He lights it with his own before passing it on to Chandresh.

Chandresh thanks the man before drawing on the *beedi*, relishing its unrefined flavour for a change.

"So, what are you nosing around here for?"

The old man clearly believes in getting to the point!

Chandresh decides that being honest and upfront will have the best pay-offs under the circumstances.

"My name is Chandresh Rajan. I am a journalist and I write on serious social and development issues, focusing on the marginalized communities in particular."

The old man stares into Chandresh's eyes as he comments bluntly.

"You probably get paid well for your efforts and maybe get some awards even. Not much comfort for the people whose miseries you bare in print!"

Chandresh realizes that he will have to earn the man's respect if he hopes to get him to speak.

"They would have no comfort even otherwise. I am not saying that I have achieved very much but please give me credit at least for the effort."

The man looks at him thoughtfully before giving a small nod.

"It is the way I earn a living. So yes, I do get paid decent if not great money. And yes, it does feel good when my efforts are recognized. But in the process, along with my efforts, I am hoping the issues that I write about also get noticed."

Chandresh wonders if his justifications are meant to appease the old man or reassure himself. He does, in fact, often have moments of self-doubt, when his efforts seem futile and even selfish, but none had managed to veer him off course yet.

"So, are you here to do a story on the movement?"

Chandresh's thoughts are broken by the old man's question.

He nods in assent before clarifying.

"Yes, I am, in fact, waiting for Murthy, the local fertilizer agent, to escort me to meet the leadership."

The old man's prickly stance seems to soften just a bit. Clearly, the fact that he has earned the trust of the leadership enough to be granted an interview counts for something.

"What if I told you I was once part of a *dalam*[3] too? That I was with none other than Chotanna!"

Chandresh is a bit startled. Chotanna is a local Maoist legend, a folk hero, almost, in these parts. A high profile leader of the Maoist movement in Andhra Pradesh, he used to be a follower of Kondapalli Sitaramiah, one of India's best known Communist ideologues. Chotanna's heroics—before he was shot dead by the police in the late 1990s—had reams of newsprint devoted to them.

"I am sure you weren't a reporter already by then. But have you heard of the Gurtedu kidnappings?"

Chandresh nods vigorously. The old man is referring to an incident that occurred almost three decades ago. The Maoists had daringly kidnapped a contingent of government officials who were on a site visit to inspect the check dam that had been built at Bodlanka, a small village

---

3   A group of Naxalites—usually sixteen people—that functions and travels as an integrated unit.

on the Rampachodavaram hills in the East Godavari district of Andhra Pradesh.

"Of course I have, sir. I even know one of the IAS officers from the contingent that was kidnapped!"

"Yes, some of them must hold senior positions in the government now."

By mutual, unspoken consent, neither of them takes names.

"It was the winter of 1987 and I was part of Chottanna's *dalam* in Maredumilli in Rampachodavaram. We heard that a big contingent of government officials were to visit Bodlanka. I don't know if you have been there but Bodlanka is a beautiful village, as beautiful as its tribal inhabitants. We planned on making a strike."

The old man pauses to take a breath. The word strike confuses Chandresh.

"So, was the plan to kill them all? Did you have to change your plans and kidnap them instead?"

"No, their deaths would not have served our purpose. They were to be held hostage, in return for the release of our comrades who were imprisoned for having murdered money-lending rogues who were exploiting the poor."

Chandresh cannot help but think that the issue has remained the same over time, with only the exploitative elements acquiring a different form.

"Bodlanka used to be no man's land and no officer worth his name would ever attempt to visit this deeply inaccessible place for fear of us Annas, or Maoists as we are called by the outsiders. But some foolhardy officers decided to test the waters and we kidnapped them all in Gurtedu."

"So, were you successful in achieving your objective?"

The old man wears an expression of deep pride as he nods. His eyes twinkle as he recalls the satisfaction they derived from their success.

"We got 13 of our comrades released in exchange for the lives of seven officers—brave men who had, between them, liquidated at least 27 moneylenders who had been exploiting and harassing the tribals in the Maredumilli area. In the time that they stayed with us, we worked on sensitizing the officers on the havoc that the moneylenders had caused. I think we succeeded because a few of them carried forth our message to the people at large!"

Age might have rendered him incapable of physical participation but it is obvious that the old man's commitment remains unshaken. But of course, that is the way it is, Chandresh thinks to himself. These men are converts for life, more often than not!

"Thank you so much for sharing all of this with me. If you trust me enough, can you tell me what brought you into the folds of the Maoist movement? Was it purely ideological or was there a stronger, personal reason?"

The old man's face takes on a faraway expression. There is also a look of immense sadness on his face. When he speaks, however, his voice lacks any emotion.

"It was 2 November 1984. Indira Gandhi had been assassinated by her own security guards just two days earlier. My family and I were staying on the fields of a landlord and tending to it on his behalf. The landlord was originally a mahajan, or moneylender. He had slowly grabbed large tracts of tribal land through manipulative and coercive means. He would lend money to tribals for agriculture or other purposes, at very high rates of interest, take away their produce as interest, and value it at low rates. He lent them more and more money and eventually took away their land, leaving them indebted and vulnerable."

Chandresh feels suddenly weary and powerless. How many times had he heard this story? And each time, he could not help being gripped by the same sense of helpless outrage.

The old man seems fully aware of his story's impact on Chandresh.

"The exploitation did not stop there. He would force the female members of those indebted families, and children, to entertain him and his friends at their weekend parties, which were also attended by corrupt officers and police officials. One day, when I returned from the field, neither my wife nor my 12-year-old daughter was home. They rarely used to go out, so I was grabbed by a sudden fear. I ran to the landlord's house at the far end of the field to seek his help to find them. To my deep shock, I saw my wife and daughter leaving his home in a distraught state. They were both bruised and their clothes were in tatters. They did not survive the ordeal. Within two days, my wife killed my daughter before committing suicide herself. I walked around the village like a mad man for the next month or so. The only thing that kept me alive was my quest for justice. I knew that I would never get justice if I went to the police or the judiciary. So I chose to go to Chotanna instead. I joined his *dalam* and became a foot soldier in the battle against exploitation and social inequity. It took me two years before

I managed to secure justice for my wife and child, and I did it with my own hands! In January 1986, while the landlord and his friends were returning to Rampachodavaram from Rajahmundry, we kidnapped them all, beheaded them and placed their heads on posts in the main marketplace in Rampachodavaram. Not only was this justice for my own family but for all those who had gone through a similar ordeal. It was also a warning signal to all those who believed that they could get away with exploiting the poor. Three of my colleagues from that incident were arrested in August 1986. The Gurtedu kidnappings were to secure the release of those brave men among others."

From experience, Chandresh knows that anything he says will sound trite under the circumstances. The old man seems to have exhausted his quota of words too. They remain seated in companionable silence for a while, both drawing on their *beedis* almost in tandem.

Chandresh knows the man will be deeply insulted if he offers him money. He was not out to barter his grief for gain. And yet, he feels it would be churlish to walk away with nothing more than a handshake.

"Can I buy you another cup of tea?"

The old man's eyes twinkle.

"No more tea but maybe I could bum a cigarette off you in return?"

Chandresh's jaw drops. The sly old fox had known all along!

He sheepishly hands over the pack of cigarettes that he fishes out of his pocket.

The old man smiles at him benignly.

"Please do continue with your efforts. No matter if you don't always get results."

As Chandresh offers to shake hands in a final goodbye, the old man shakes his head. He places his hand on his forehead and offers the traditional greeting.

"Lal Salaam!"

CHAPTER 8

The villagers watch open-mouthed. It is like a scene from the movies—a Vijayashanthi movie, to be specific! Except that Vijayashanthi[4] is almost always in uniform and beats the villains to pulp. Muscle flexing is not this petite, feisty young woman's style, though. Veena Mehra, the newly appointed district magistrate of Ranga Reddy district, means business. As she eyeballs the evil landlord into submitting to her authority, the small crowd lets out a cheer. The noise becomes deafening when she escorts Rajayya to her official jeep. A bonded labourer for 33 out of his 40 years, he is free at last!

More than half a century after India achieved its independence, the practice of bonded labour as a form of modern slavery continues to exist. The economically

---

4   Well-known Indian actress who often performs macho roles in Telugu and Tamil films.

backward Ranga Reddy district has always found itself in the eye of this controversy. When news of Veena Mehra assuming office as DM broke, those who knew of her tough stance against all forms of exploitation found reason to celebrate. On her part, immediately upon taking over, she promised to act on an ILO-sponsored report containing 30 bonded labour case studies in the district.

Rajayya's father had been a bonded labourer too; it was a family tradition. With no fixed or movable assets, the only thing of value he had to pledge at the time of a financial crisis, was the family's physical labour. Rajayya was first pledged to the landlord at the age of seven for a sum of Rs 25,000 and was given the responsibility of grazing the landlord's cattle. He was paid a nominal salary of Rs 50 per year. While it took ten years to repay the original loan, the family had taken more loans to pay for weddings, funerals, illnesses and the like, in the interim. As a result, Rajayya was never a free man. Not until the government, in the form of Veena Mehra, intervened, that is!

Watching Rajayya leave her office with his family after repeatedly expressing his gratitude, Veena feels a quite a sense of satisfaction. This feeling is one of the perks of her job, to be revisited every time circumstances or forces beyond her control challenge or frustrate her. The challenges and frustrations definitely outnumber the scattered moments of contentment. Yet, it is the latter that make her efforts seem worthwhile. Despite belonging to what can be described as a privileged, high-caste background, she has always been a firm believer in the universal right to human dignity. After a degree in electronics engineering from the prestigious

Indian Institute of Technology (IIT), Bombay, she chose to enter the Indian Administrative Service (IAS), when most of her colleagues were jetting off to foreign shores in pursuit of higher education or other opportunities.

While securing a man's freedom is a worthy task in itself, it does not completely resolve the problem at hand. The government can exert its authority in releasing those who are in bondage and even punish those who have been oppressing them, but the larger issue of lack of access to resources and the resultant indebtedness remains. With no other resource but their own physical labour from which to eke out a living, the poor are forced to turn to their employers at the time of financial need. The employers, be they landlords, brick kiln or factory owners, make good use of the opportunity to extract cheap labour and keep them bound to them for years at length.

While the government and other agencies have tried to tackle this very need for livelihood opportunities, a steady income source and access to finance in emergencies through a variety of schemes, each of them has had its own share of attendant problems.

Veena's mind goes back to the call that she had received from the Principal Secretary (Rural Development, GoAP), MR, just a couple of days ago.

"Your favourite bête noire is causing havoc yet again!"

While Veena had an inkling of what he was referring to, she had wanted to make sure just in case.

"Sir, there are so many of them that I have lost count. Which one are you referring to?"

"You are among the few sincere and straightforward

officers we have, Veena. So yes, the bête noires are many. But this one is surely special. This one had you winning a Presidential medal when your opponents were hoping you would be suspended in disgrace!"

Veena could not resist a dry smile, though she knew MR would have no way of seeing her expression.

MR had been referring to the Krishna Crisis[5], of course. It was one of her earliest battles, coming within a year of her first posting as District Magistrate of Krishna District. Although her family originally hailed from Bhopal in Madhya Pradesh, they had moved to Andhra Pradesh more than three generations ago. She had been more than happy when she had been allotted to serve in Andhra Pradesh after being inducted into the IAS cadre.

Veena's grandfather had always teased her saying that she had a penchant for drama. Or, maybe, drama had a penchant for her. She had made her entry into the world on a stormy night, complete with lightning flashes and thunder bolts. Ever since then, things were always happening around her or she was where things were happening. Her first assignment as DM was quite a dramatic one too. Located between the Krishna and the Godavari delta, the Kolleru Lake is the second largest fresh water lake in the state of Andhra Pradesh. Almost 15,000 acres of the lake had been encroached upon by the land mafia. Veena had headed the

---

5   In 2005–6, the microfinance sector in Andhra Pradesh was subject to a huge crisis in the Krishna and neighbouring Guntur districts and many allegations were made against MFIs with regard to charging of high interest rates, use of coercive repayment tactics, over-lending, physical abuse of clients, etc.

Kolleru operation, which took on the might of the local heavyweight politicians who were part of the land mafia.

Veena further initiated "Palle Nidra", an innovative programme that involved making a night halt at villages along with officials and public representatives. It was during one such halt that Veena had come to know certain unsavoury truths regarding the MFIs operating in the area. Truths that led to the ballooning of what has been described as the Krishna crisis. It was a curious case of protectors turning predators. There were three major complaints against the MFIs operating there: one, that they were charging exorbitantly high rates of interest, ranging from 40 to 60 per cent per annum; the second was that they were abusing human rights by detaining relatives of defaulters or suggesting to them that the borrower commit suicide so they could claim the insurance money; and three, that they were creating large-scale rural indebtedness.

Yet another key reason that triggered off the Krishna crisis was the rivalry between the public sector bank-supported SHG Bank linkage programme, funded by an international donor and the Andhra Pradesh government, and the private sector MFIs, funded by robust private sector and foreign banks. Keen to show better results, the MFIs had adopted a variety of underhand and anti-client measures to boost their profits. The spate of suicides was the reason why their unsavoury and illegal activities were exposed, leading to their suspension. Interestingly the suicides, as a consequence of indebtedness, started increasing from 2006, when the state government started encouraging the growth of MFIs as an alternative to public sector banks. MFIs had shown scant regard for the laws of the state while lending to the poor and they often flaunted their certificates of registration with the Federal Banking Regulator to prevent any action by the state government.

During one of her visits to the villages, Veena had met the family of Victoria, who had pledged her ration card and then the *mangalsutra* of her newly married daughter with an MFI in order to meet emergency expenses. This was in gross violation of the FBR norms which prohibited MFIs from taking collateral for the loans provided under the microcredit category. Subsequently, the MFI recovery agents had applied severe pressure on Victoria to make repayments and, finding herself unable to meet their demands, she had committed suicide.

An infuriated Veena had raided the offices of many MFIs in the region, including Aashray, DevEx and Sowmya, among others, and had charged them with collection of higher interest rates, almost to the tune of 40 per cent, and for harassing borrowers. In the process of the raids, they had also unearthed signed blank demand promissory notes at many of their premises.

There was also evidence of Aashray and DevEx, two competing MFIs, indulging in sleazy and underhand tactics in order to undercut each other. Aashray had tried to disrupt the operations of DevEx by plying the husbands of their field staff with liquor. This way, they hoped, the husbands would not allow their wives to perform their roles effectively. When DevEx officers learned of this, they retaliated by supplying the male field staff of Aashray with sex workers. Veena had been left disgusted by the happenings and, more so, by the blatant disregard most of these MFIs had for the welfare of the very clients they were mandated to serve. Following this, she had ordered shut more than fifty branches of the MFIs in the district.

Refusing to be cowed down, the MFIs had launched a counter-offensive against Veena by lodging a complaint against her with the Chief Minister. They alleged that she had behaved in a high-handed manner and had not complied with proper procedures before shutting down their branches. They had also insinuated that she was colluding with the banks to cut them out of the supply chain.

The fight between the MFIs on the one hand and the people and administration of the Krishna district on the other, was of particular consequence because of its possible impact on the course of microfinance elsewhere in the country. For one, just four districts of Andhra (Krishna, West Godavari, Guntur and Prakasam) accounted for about 15 per cent of all micro-loans in the country. The success of the Andhra Pradesh model was what had sold microfinance as an idea to the rest of the country. Many of the MFIs were slowly branching out to other states like Tamil Nadu, Maharashtra and the northern "BIMARU" states—Bihar, Madhya Pradesh, Rajasthan and Uttar Pradesh.

As a consequence of the Krishna crisis, which saw caps on interest rates, loan write-offs and stringent regulations being imposed, the microfinance sector in Andhra experienced a slowdown. Banks, too, were increasingly unwilling to lend to the MFIs as a result. It was around the same time that many private equity and venture capital funds started evincing an interest in investing in microfinance. Wall Street's entry was undoubtedly seen as a game changer.

Veena was given a clean chit by the enquiry committee set up to investigate the allegations made against her by the MFIs, and was subsequently awarded the President's Gold Medal for exemplary service. Wherever she was transferred after that, she always kept an ear to the ground for news on the activities of MFIs in the region. It saddened her to see the sector once again possessed by the ghost of suicides as MFIs returned to their old ways of coercion and oversupply of credit. Similar news was pouring in from other districts too, as she found out during her interaction with her peers.

The knock on the door brings Veena to the present.

"Yes, come in!"

Her PA, Nilanjan, enters with a file in hand.

"Madam, we have a detailed report of all the incidents in our district."

"Five of them, right?"

"Six in all, Madam! There was a suicide reported last night. And there have been two kidnappings, where the daughters of the indebted women have been held captive as a means to coerce them into repaying their debts."

"Have they been rescued since?"

"The girl from Parichemam village has been rescued, Madam. She was found locked up in an old warehouse about 5 km from the village. The warehouse is said to belong to a local politician whose relative works as a collection agent with SAMMAAN. The police are still trying to find the whereabouts of the other girl."

Veena is infuriated by this news.

"Scratch the surface of most instances of such exploitation and you find some kind of political sanction! Four years have passed and the sector's conscience continues to be in hibernation."

Veena gets up with a start.

"Call the SP and inform him that I am headed to Parichemam. I want to speak to that girl myself. I am not stopping until we get to the bottom of this and gather enough evidence against SAMMAAN. There can be no better time to push for action."

Veena's phone rings as she rushes out of the room.

"Good morning, sir!"

"Are you on the job, Veena?"

"You will have a report on your desk in the next half an hour, Sir. I am personally headed to investigate a case of coercion by SAMMAAN. I will get you enough evidence to nail them, Sir. I only hope there is no interference from the higher-ups this time."

"It might be a little tough to step back this time, Veena. This is no Krishna crisis but rather a crisis for the whole state, with consequences for the nation and beyond."

CHAPTER 9

HYDERABAD, 1 OCTOBER 2010

Bob knows he is severely jetlagged but wonders if he is beginning to hallucinate as well. Is his mind conjuring up images of the things he desperately seeks? He had spent all his waking hours on the flight from New York to Mumbai reading up the James Jordin report and mulling over the insightful revelations made by Tom Moody during their brief chat. Then there was the interview with a senior executive director at the Federal Banking Regulator, in charge of microfinance operations, before the flight to Hyderabad. Bob is fairly certain that his brain is suffering from a microfinance overload. Why else would Chandresh Rajan be strolling into the coffee shop of his hotel?

It is only when Chandresh walks up to his table and shakes his hand rather vigorously that Bob is convinced that he is for real.

"Bob, I am truly glad to finally meet you in person."

"Chan, you've risen from the dead at last! I have lost count of the number of times I've tried calling you."

"You'll have to forgive me for that, Bob. The thing is, I have had no network for almost two weeks now. I got back into town just last night and saw your detailed email and travel itinerary. I thought I'd come by and not spoil the surprise with a phone call."

"Surprise? More like shock! I was wondering if my jetlagged, overwrought mind had conjured you up!"

Chandresh laughs before taking a seat across the table from Bob.

The waiter comes to check if he would like breakfast.

"Why don't you, Chan? Their spread is pretty good."

"Thanks Bob, but I'll pass. No cooked food for me till lunch. Wouldn't mind some coffee, though."

Chandresh orders his coffee. The waiter nods in acknowledgment before hurrying away.

"So, something exciting that you've been working on?", asks Bob.

"Exciting? I am not sure I would use that word. But yes, it was a challenging opportunity."

Chandresh seems hesitant about divulging details.

"I think I have embarked on a challenging mission too. To verify if all that glitters is indeed gold!"

Chandresh laughs.

"So, is Kamineni the only gold you are after?"

"Not really. Although this journey sort of began with him. I got to meet him at the CIRIG office in Boston last week. And I should be meeting him again in...."

Bob looks at his wristwatch before adding,

"...about an hour from now."

Chandresh raises his eyebrows.

"Of course, the big man will bend over backwards to please you, given the publication you represent. His biggest fans are from your part of the world, after all."

Bob's eyes gleam with amusement.

"Do I detect a sour note? I guess you both are not the best of pals?"

Chandresh grins broadly.

"Far from it! But be warned, you may become persona non grata by the time you are done. He used to be ultra polite with me too, in a different life."

Bob shrugs.

"We're not here to make friends anyway. So, does that mean you won't go with me to the SAMMAAN office?"

"Poor Kamineni. Let us not put his diplomatic skills to such great test!"

Chandresh throws back his head and laughs. Just then, his phone rings and he excuses himself to take the call.

Bob drains the coffee from his cup before checking his watch again.

"Come on, let's go!"

Bob looks up in surprise.

"You mean you're going with me? I thought you..."

"Breaking news, there has been a fire at the SAMMAAN office!"

Bob is shocked.

"What are you saying? How did it happen? Was it an accident or some kind of arson?"

"You came here for a soft news story. Looks like you'll be reporting hard news instead."

Bob is still befuddled as he follows Chandresh out of the café.

———*∿∿∿*———

The steel and glass façade of the SAMMAAN office is covered in smoke and soot. The fire brigade has left but one can see the remnants of their efforts in the form of puddles all over the place. The police are having a hard time keeping the jostling media out of the way as experts try to investigate the cause of the tragedy.

For it is now a tragedy that has consumed three lives. Among the dead are a security guard, a junior accountant and Sridevi, executive assistant to Prasad Kamineni. While the accountant was already dead by the time the rescue team broke in, the other two died on the way to the hospital. The cause of death in all three cases appeared to be asphyxiation.

Even as the media try their best to enter the premises and get first-hand information on what has transpired, Prasad Kamineni is seen emerging from the building. The man is clearly distraught and is supported by two of his staff members. As he walks out, the media breaks through the police cordon and surges ahead with mikes and cameras in hand.

Chaos prevails for a few seconds before the police step in to restore order. The journalists, however, are not to be deterred.

"Mr Kamineni, how did the fire break out?"

"Do you suspect arson or foul play?"

"What do you have to say about the deaths?"

Kamineni raises his hand, requesting silence.

"It is my duty to answer all your questions. If I can take them one by one, please? Before that, I would like to say a few words myself."

The journalists quieten down and wait for Kamineni to continue.

"I do not know what or who caused the fire. That is something that the police investigation will reveal. The culprits, if any, will certainly be brought to book soon. I have made a humble request to the Police Commissioner on the matter. However, whatever may be the cause, I accept complete responsibility for this tragedy on behalf of SAMMAAN. I have personally suffered the loss of three employees, one of whom was practically a sister to me. I am grieving like any other family member would. I want to announce an ex-gratia payment of one million rupees to the families of each of those we have lost. Money can never make up for this loss but I hope it will contribute to the futures of the children they have left behind."

"Considering the killing he made by selling his shares just ahead of the IPO, he can afford to pay this and more!"

Bob overhears a senior journalist's remark to one of his colleagues. He turns to look at Chandresh who merely shrugs. Clearly, Kamineni's remorse, genuine or otherwise, is not cutting ice.

"Mr Kamineni, apparently the fire started around 6 am. What were your executive assistant and the office accountant doing here that early?"

Kamineni looks stricken.

"I am afraid I must take the blame for that. We have an

AGM coming up in three days' time. We were supposed to get a lot of paperwork ready for that. In fact, I was due to join them myself. I was on my way when my car broke down. I called for a cab and was waiting for it to arrive when I was informed about the fire. I rushed here in the first autorickshaw I could find. When I got here, there was nothing to be done."

"A hollow excuse if ever I have heard one."

The senior journalist mutters yet again before raising his hand.

"Mr Kamineni, do you think this fire has anything to do with the series of microfinance-related suicides the state has been witnessing? If my sources are right, at least seven of the reported cases were clients of SAMMAAN."

Kamineni turns sharply towards the journalist. He sees Bob and Chandresh standing beside him. It is gone in the fraction of a second but Bob catches an expression of anger mixed with consternation on Kamineni's face.

"Sir, both are terrible tragedies. I would not like to link one to the other. Certainly not before the police have had time to investigate. However, with regard to the suicides, I would like to reiterate that SAMMAAN does not resort to arm-twisting or any other illegal debt-recovery practices. If there have been suicides, they have not been the result of any coercive tactics on our part. As we all know, there are around two hundred thousand reported cases of suicide in India every year."

The police indicate that the media wind up their interrogation. As Kamineni is escorted to his car, he stops to greet Bob and Chandresh.

"I am so sorry we are meeting again under such unfortunate circumstances, Bob."

"I am really sorry too, Prasad, but accidents happen."

"Yes Bob, they do."

Kamineni greets Chandresh.

"Chandresh..."

"Unfortunate thing to have happened, Prasad...I can see how personally you've taken it."

"Of course, I have lost three members of my family today."

Chandresh nods as he places his hand on Prasad's shoulder.

Kamineni turns back to Bob.

"Bob, you must excuse me for today. Give me a day or two to get a grip on myself. We can then meet and discuss things at length."

"Of course, Prasad, you have a lot to attend to now. Please do not worry about me! I am planning to visit various MFIs in different districts of AP to gather a grassroots-level understanding of the state of the sector. We could certainly speak once I return. But, in the meantime, it would be great if your office can facilitate interactions with your staff and clientele across the branches."

"Certainly, Bob. Just mail us a travel plan in terms of which districts you intend on visiting and when. My office will make sure that you get all the support you need. Have you made arrangements for transport and other things? We would be happy to spare you one of our vehicles, and one of our staff could accompany you too."

"Very kind of you to offer, Prasad, particularly under

the circumstances. But Chandresh is making all the arrangements. We will be travelling together.

Kamineni smiles faintly.

"You have the best possible guide, then. He probably knows more about the grassroots goings-on than any of us. But I am sure you will make your own assessment."

"Of course, Prasad, we journalists have multiple sources but the ultimate assessment remains ours."

"But of course."

Kamineni nods at both men before walking towards his car.

"He does seem visibly disturbed."

Chandresh shrugs.

"I am still wondering what they were really doing here at daybreak."

"He did say something about an annual general body meeting."

"He did. I can even understand the accountant, but why Kamineni's executive assistant?"

Bob looks at Chandresh contemplatively.

"Yet another question that begs to be answered!"

CHAPTER 10

Ramaiyya wakes up to a headache and an itchy throat—a clear sign that he has gone without a drink for too long. He slowly sits up, holding his pounding head in his hands. It is dark all around him save for the streaks of sunlight leaking through the cracks in the roof.

The dilapidated structure used to be a cattle shed and a residual odour still lingers in the air. Ramaiyya idly wonders which is worse—the pungent smell or the oppressive heat caused by the asbestos sheets on the roof. The place is now a hideout for Bhava Reddy's men. The land belongs to Bhava himself, a follower of political strongman Nageswara Reddy.

Ramaiyya has been working for Bhava Reddy for almost a decade. An erstwhile history-sheeter with interests ranging from illicit liquor to brothels, Bhava had acquired a veneer of respectability after he joined politics some six years ago. After a fair bit of party hopping, he finally settled down in Nageshwara Reddy's

84

party. Meanwhile, his other activities continued. The baton was merely passed on to Bhava Reddy's nephew, Chiranjeevi. The nephew proved a worthy successor by expanding his uncle's repertoire to include various other activities such as extortion and kidnapping.

In the general elections held the previous year, Nageshwara Reddy's party had won enough parliamentary seats to merit a presence in the coalition that now held the reins of power at the centre. Bhava Reddy's clout and connections, in addition to the generous handouts, had ensured that the district police force turned a blind eye to their activities for a long time, but the ascension to power tilted the scales even further in their favour. Bhava Reddy and his band of men developed a stronger sense of entitlement.

A huge feeling of resentment seizes Ramaiyya as he thinks back to the events of the last few days and, more importantly, the part played by DM Veena Mehra. The woman had been a thorn in their side ever since she had taken charge of the district three months ago.

It had begun with a raid on one of their distilleries; then there was the freeing of a bonded labourer who worked on the lands of one of the party benefactors. And now, the crackdown on the loan recovery operations of SAMMAAN Microfinance. Chiranjeevi often assisted these operations on the insistence of his wife Jamuna, whose cousin, Gopal Reddy worked as a loan recovery agent with SAMMAAN.

Their last operation had been the abduction of two girls from his village, Parichemam, to coerce their parents into settling the multiple loans they had taken, and the instalments for which had been more than six months overdue. They had taken both the girls to an old, unused warehouse that 'belonged' to Bhava Reddy. Ramaiyya and his team took turns to guard the warehouse while negotiations were on with the parents.

Ramaiyya had expected the operation to go smoothly, as it almost always did. The parents would pay up and the girls would be returned safely. But DM Veena Mehra and her dogged determination upset all his plans. She organized a special police party to rescue the girls; the team raided the warehouse where the girls had been held captive and even managed to free one of them.

Ramaiyya had not been there at the time of the raid. It was his younger son's birthday and he had gone home to be with him. After stuffing his face with the spicy fish curry his wife had cooked, Ramaiyya had fallen asleep. He was in the middle of a dream involving a buxom film heroine when his wife's scream jolted him out of it.

"Run, before the cops get here! They have rescued Gomti's daughter from the warehouse. The DM is coming here to speak to her. She is bound to identify you!"

For a moment Ramaiyya had not been sure which to rue more—the abrupt end to his fantasy or the girl's rescue. Then he regained his wits and scrammed.

It had been four days since. He had gone straight to Chiranjeevi's house and was directed to hide in the old cow shed nearby. He assumed that the police would sniff around for just a few days. But clearly, the DM had other plans.

Ramaiyya curses under his breath. Who decided that women should be educated and occupy positions of power?

The bitch probably fancied herself as some film heroine out to serve justice to the poor!

Ramaiyya sits up with a start as he hears the door creak open. He heaves a sigh of relief when he sees that it is his wife, carrying a tiffin. He realizes he has not eaten a morsel in almost eight hours. Feeling ravenous, he grabs the tiffin and starts stuffing his face with food.

"Have you brought my liquor too?"

"Today is Gandhi Jayanti, the liquor shops are all closed."

Ramaiyya curses under his breath.

"I met the DM last night."

Ramaiyya almost spits out the food in his mouth.

"What...what are you talking about?"

"I met Veena Madam ji last night. She alone can save—"

Ramaiyya slaps her hard across her face. Either the woman is immune to his violence or he is losing his strength for she hardly flinches.

"Are you crazy? I don't need any saving! I have my bosses to take care of my safety, they are the ones that have put a roof over our heads!"

"Enough of your nonsense. Your bosses may have paid for the booze that courses through your veins, but they certainly haven't kept my children or me from cold or hunger. If it weren't for my snacks stall, we would all be out on the streets."

"Enough of your drama! You talk too much only because you have a few pennies in your hand. Let me just get out of here, I'm going to send you back to your parents' home!"

"When you get out of here, you are going straight to prison and nowhere else."

"So you went and pleaded with the DM to set her cops after me? Revealed my whereabouts, have you?"

"I might have, if you hadn't been the father of my children. But I didn't want them to be orphaned!"

Ramaiyya is on the verge of losing patience. Part of him just wants to push her aside and get away, maybe go to the Municipal Councillor's house, ask for some money and escape to the city for a while.

Almost as if she can read his mind, his wife says, "Don't waste your time making plans. Bhava Reddy has been suspended from the party on disciplinary grounds. He is too busy saving his own skin to bother about yours!"

Ramaiyya is now a worried man.

"How do you know all this?"

"The farmhand working on their lands told his wife and she told me. That is why I went rushing to the DM last night."

"How did you find her? You couldn't have just walked into her house!"

"I can and I did. Now just shut up and listen to what happened."

———※———

Would the DM help her husband? Or was she unwittingly laying a trap for him herself?

This thought was uppermost in Vijaya's mind as she waited outside the DM's bungalow. It helped that she knew the guard on duty; his niece was an acquaintance of hers.

Seeing her plight, he had taken pity on her and agreed to inform the DM of her request for an audience.

He had been gone for almost ten minutes. And Vijaya had just begun to wonder if she was better off leaving, when he came rushing back.

"DM Madam has asked me to bring you in. Come now, be quick!"

Vijaya practically ran into the bungalow with the old guard struggling to keep pace with her.

The cook escorted her to the reception area and pointed towards a sofa in a corner. Vijaya was too overwhelmed to even consider sitting. The man shrugged and left.

Vijaya mentally rehearsed her lines. Hardly five minutes later, when the DM walked into the room and nodded at her, all thoughts fled Vijaya's mind. She was sure she would not be able to get even a word out. Luckily for her, the DM was talking on her phone and probably didn't notice her expression.

"Okay *beta*, finish your homework quickly now and I will ask your dad to take you to the movies over the weekend."

Vijaya had not been able to comprehend much of her conversation, but her tone and the mention of homework made her conclude that she was probably talking to her child. The thought made Veena seem a little less intimidating. She was a mother too, just like her. She would surely understand Vijaya's concern for her children.

"Yes...what did you want to see me about?"

Her tone was authoritative and impersonal. Vijaya felt tears springing to her eyes. At a loss for words, she did the only thing that she could think of.

Veena Mehra was visibly taken aback when Vijaya prostrated herself before her.

"Hey...get up now...I don't appreciate this kind of behaviour!"

Vijaya could not control herself any more. She started crying loudly.

Veena quickly summoned her assistant and asked him to help her up. The man hesitated and Vijaya shrunk back, reminding Veena about the sensitive gender dynamics in the village. She asked him to get Vijaya some water and helped her up. The kindness made Vijaya cry harder. Finally, after much protest, Veena managed to make her sit on a chair opposite hers.

"It's okay. Just take a deep breath to calm yourself."

The cook had entered with a bottle of water and Vijaya quickly gulped the contents.

"Would you like a cup of coffee?"

Vijaya shook her head vehemently.

Veena motioned for the cook to leave before turning to Vijaya, looking at her intently.

"Why do I get the feeling I have seen you somewhere?"

Vijaya was taken aback. She had been on the fringes of the crowd that had gathered around Gomti's house when Veena had come visiting. Veena had spent almost an hour talking to Gomti's daughter, Varalakshmi, one of the two abducted girls. The crowd had listened spellbound as she gently assured the girl and her mother of support and protection from the administration. It was the manner in which she spoke to them that had convinced Vijaya to seek her help.

"Amma, you had come to our Parichemam village...to meet Varalakshmi."

"Wait, weren't you the woman who kept ducking every time you caught my eye?"

Vijaya squirmed in her seat as she realized that her attempts to avoid being noticed had resulted in the reverse. Not that it mattered now.

"Amma, please help me...my children need their father!"

Vijaya poured her heart out to her. Her unhappy and abusive marriage and their four children, Ramaiyya' history and how he had never paid heed to her fervent pleas to give up his violent ways for the sake of the children, the fact that Ramaiyya had been working closely with Chiranjeevi and his relative, who had spearheaded the SAMMAAN operations in the area and was responsible for many cases of kidnapping and extortion, including the latest kidnapping of the two girls from Parichemam. She begged Veena to grant her husband a pardon, and promised that he'd surrender himself and offer to turn witness to prove the coercive tactics adopted by SAMMAAN.

Veena listened patiently before finally telling Vijaya that Ramaiyya would have to face punishment for his actions. However, if he did turn witness, she could request the authorities to take a slightly more lenient view of his actions. She promised Vijaya to help with their children's education.

Vijaya fell at her feet again to thank her for her generosity and kindness.

Ramaiyya feels a nagging headache coming on as his wife continues to sing the DM's praises. He resists a strong urge to wring her neck, just to make her stop. She seems to have developed some connections that might just come in handy.

"I need some time to think."

Vijaya looks at him like he is a mad man.

"Are you crazy? There is no more time to think. You don't have any other option!"

Ramaiyya gnashes his teeth. The woman is clearly feeling bold after her tryst with the DM.

"Don't tell me what I have and what I don't. I have listened patiently to all that you have had to say. Now I need time to think and make my decision. Even if you run the family, I am still the man of the house!"

Ramaiyya pulls out the bundle of *beedis* tucked into his waistband. There is only one left. He curses under his breath.

"Get me a bundle of *beedis*," he says, pushing Vijaya away. "I need tobacco to kick-start my brain."

She looks at him beseechingly.

"I beg of you! Come with me to the DM now. She will keep you safe."

"Scoot now before I give you another blow!"

She leaves reluctantly, repeatedly turning back to look at him pleadingly.

Ramaiyya wonders if the woman has a point after all. It might be his best option, even if for a while.

CHAPTER 11

Bob's eyes keep straying towards the ceiling—at least a dozen times in the hour they have spent in the tiny house. His distracted behaviour can be blamed only in part on the fact that the conversation happening around him is in an alien language. He cannot shy away from the fact that he is in the grip of morbid fascination. He is, after all, sitting under the very same roof that a poor woman had hung herself from less than a month ago. All because Mylaram Kavala had not been able to repay a debt that ran into a few hundred dollars. Paradoxically, she had been one of the beneficiaries of what Wall Street considered a gilt-edged investment. Over 800 million dollars had been poured into an industry that the investor community thrived on even as recession broke the backbone of the world economy. And yet it was also what killed Mylaram Kavala, or at least that is what her daughter, Kala believed.

Bob wonders if he is being a tad too melodramatic. Even

93

so, there is no escaping from the truth behind the almost poignant display of emotion that they have just witnessed. The microfinance industry had indeed killed Mylaram Kavala. It kept pressing loan after loan into her hands, with hardly any thought to her capacity to absorb or repay. As it had done with numerous other women like her, if their research over the last few days was anything to go by.

Bob cannot help feeling shocked as he recalls the sheer impunity with which rules appear to have been flouted across institutions. When they had left Hyderabad in the rented SUV, Chandresh had suggested sampling the operations of SAMMAAN, DevEx, Aashray and Sowmya, the four major microfinance institutions in Andhra Pradesh across the districts of Ranga Reddy, Mehboob Nagar, Medak, Warangal, Krishna and Guntur. Since the highest number of suicides had been reported from Ranga Reddy district, they had decided to begin their research there. Despite Prasad Kamineni's smooth assurances, Bob had observed that the branch officers at SAMMAAN and the field-level staff were not too eager to share information. While there was no open hostility, he had observed a marked reluctance to share records, a tendency to obfuscate or gloss over details whenever Chandresh pointed out or questioned any discrepancies or lack of information. Despite the language barrier that made Bob rely heavily on Chandresh, it had not been impossible for him to see through their avoidance tactics and shifty body language.

Every such visit confirmed their niggling suspicions; in fact, things turned out to be much worse than they had imagined. It soon became obvious that SAMMAAN was not alone in its methods. There were definite trends across institutions indicating a broader malaise that affected the sector as a whole.

Chandresh had shared with Bob that he had been hearing rumbles from the ground for some time now. It had seemed to Chandresh that the microfinance industry in the state was headed for yet another fall, the triggers for which had been the consequences of the 2006 Krishna crisis. The drying up of funds from public sector sources after the Krishna crisis had resulted in the industry turning heavily towards the profit motive-driven private sector. The resultant emphasis on bottom lines and profits had seen the MFIs violate their very founding principle, which was to ensure access to affordable finance for the poor.

Bob, in turn, spoke of his own initial reservations about the industry's fairytale growth story. An industry with a self-proclaimed commitment to poverty alleviation boasted of a phenomenal growth rate at a time when the world economy had been in the throes of recession. Global investors flocked to it like bees to a honey pot, keen to invest in what they perceived as low on risk and high on returns, with a social sector tag to boot.

The discrepancies between the records and ground level realities were damning, to say the least. Bob had been prepared for some margin of error but what they uncovered was way beyond acceptable levels. Even while acknowledging that he probably had a developed nation or a Western world bias, Bob believed India to be a land where people had scant respect for the written law and found ways to bend, if not flout, rules to suit their interests.

Since the unwritten law was to break the law, no one even batted an eyelid at any such instances. And yet, the degree of discrepancy or falsification of records observed on the ground during the field visits was indeed staggering. Almost every branch of every organization that they visited seemed to have ghost clients in their books of accounts. When Bob and Chandresh ventured into the villages, they found that the women named in the books either simply did not exist or had been long dead. In one of those instances, the SAMMAAN agent accompanying them even tried to cook up a story about initials being mistakenly interchanged, to cover their tracks. She then produced a woman who she claimed was the person named in the books. The fraud was uncovered soon enough when another MFI, Aashray, produced the same woman as their client, albeit under a different name. In another instance, while the MFI representative claimed that a client was recently deceased, her family revealed that she had been dead for more than five years. It became obvious that loans were being issued in the name of a dead woman and her family was certainly not the beneficiary.

There was also the matter of multiple lending. Almost all of the MFIs operating in a village had lent to the same clients concurrently without a thought to their credit absorption or repayment capacity, a blatant violation of the norms established by the Federal Banking Regulator. Bob and Chandresh found that the MFIs had been colluding among themselves and had even charted schedules for village visits, allotting specific days of the week to each of them so as to avoid any clashes. Later, of course, they would be unsparing in their efforts to recover their loan instalments, pushing their clients up against the wall or, in extreme cases like Mylaram Kavala's, to hang from the roofs of their homes.

"They would often tell her that she should make better use of her daughters!"

Bob's reverie is broken by Chandresh's harsh words.

Mylaram's younger daughter is sobbing softly, while the older one seems too weary for even that. She leans against a wall, her eyes vacant, drained of all emotion.

Bob turns to Chandresh.

"Chan, is she hinting at threats of sexual abuse?"

Chandresh nods grimly.

"Yeah Bob, she is. Maybe Mylaram thought they might act on their threats someday. Maybe she thought she was saving them from harm by killing herself."

Bob exhales roughly.

"She might have well made them more vulnerable. Do they have any other family? Where will these girls go? What will they do now?"

Chandresh gets up abruptly.

"I think we are done here, Bob. Let's get going."

Not quite used to squatting on the floor, Bob struggles to raise himself and takes Chandresh's outstretched hand.

"We don't have any pictures of hers to give out. You can click one if you like."

Kala points to the photograph that hangs on the wall. The garland of flowers around it is a few days old. All that remains is a sorry looking string with a few stubborn flowers that refuse to fall off, even though they are long dead. The woman in the photograph is of indefinite age and so is the expression on her face.

"Would you mind posing beside it?"

Chandresh translates Bob's request for the benefit of the girls before stepping out of the house.

The older daughter positions herself next to the picture and continues to stare at them vacantly. The younger one wipes her face clean with a towel and tries to set her hair right before she goes and stands to the other side of the picture.

Bob takes a couple of shots and nods to the girls in acknowledgement before he steps out.

Chandresh stands in the shade of a tree a few yards away, smoking a cigarette.

Bob walks towards him.

"I asked you a question in there, Chan. What of the future of these girls?"

Chandresh is silent for a moment before he replies, without looking at Bob.

"How does it matter, Bob? We have our story. Let's go looking for the next."

Bob touches his shoulder.

"Don't be so harsh on yourself."

Chandresh turns to look at him and gives him a half smile.

"You need to be strong!"

Chandresh shrugs and walks quickly towards the car.

Bob half jogs to keep up with him, wondering if he should have given the girls some money. Would they have been offended?

"How much could you have given? And how long would it have kept them? And how many of them would you give to?"

Bob is taken aback. How had Chandresh managed to read his thoughts?

"It wasn't too hard!"

Ignoring Bob's incredulous look, Chandresh opens the SUV door and gestures for Bob to get in.

Bob clambers in. Just as Chandresh is about to follow him, he is hailed by a youth running towards him.

"Sir...please wait!"

Chandresh recognizes him as Ramu, the local stringer for a regional newspaper. They had met a couple of years ago when Chandresh was working on a story on farmer suicides in the region. The boy had taken to calling him whenever he thought of a local story that might interest him or merit nationwide attention. Chandresh had spoken to him over the phone just that morning to see if he could shed any further light on the ongoing crisis.

"Hello Ramu, what are you doing here?"

"Sir, I came looking for you. Your mobile was not reachable. And you had mentioned that you were going to visit Mylaram Kavala's family."

Ramu catches his breath.

Chandresh's brows furrow in concentration. Ramu would not have come chasing after him unless he was on to something.

"Sir, you know that Sowjanya International School...that residential school on the outskirts of the town? I just heard that there was an IT raid there yesterday."

Chandresh frowns.

"On a school premises? Okay, I'll put one of the daily reporters in touch with you, Ramu. It might be of interest to them."

Ramu shakes his head frantically.

"Sir...the raid is not the point... at least not directly. The thing is, Sowjanya is owned and run by Srinivas Potluri...."

He pauses and looks at Chandresh expectantly. Chandresh is puzzled.

"So, is this Potluri some local politican?"

Ramu looks a little disappointed.

"Sir,..he is the maternal uncle of Kumudini Potluri!"

Realization dawns on Chandresh.

Of course! And Kumudini Potluri is the CEO of DevEx!

"I had no idea! So, do you expect Kumudini to use her political connections to bail her uncle out?"

"Sir, forget that...the fact is Srinivas Potluri is her front man!"

Chandresh's interest is piqued.

"Are you saying that she has other business interests besides microfinance?"

Ramu takes a deep breath before responding.

"I suspect that the school is a conduit to route money to and from DevEx."

Chandresh lets out a low whistle.

"That is a big allegation to make. I am still waiting to hear from Kumudini's office on an appointment. I'll make sure to probe in this direction if she agrees to meet me."

Ramu smiles broadly.

"That was the whole point of my coming here, sir. Kumudini Potluri is reaching the school premises as we speak."

Chandresh feels a latent excitement kick in. As a reporter, he had always enjoyed corralling reluctant subjects down and coaxing them to speak. He claps Ramu's shoulder before pumping his hand enthusiastically.

"I owe you one, Ramu!"

Ramu smiles modestly and wishes Chandresh luck before leaving.

Chandresh jumps into the SUV, eager to share the news of the lucky break with Bob.

"Bob, we've had a stroke of—"

He stops midway, on seeing that Bob is on the phone.

"Okay, please tell Maarten that I will call him within an hour, as soon as I get to the hotel. He should wait for my call...okay Priya, take care."

Bob hangs up and turns to Chandresh with a quizzical look.

Chandresh responds with a query.

"Do you have to go back to the hotel right now?"

"Wasn't that the plan anyway?"

Chandresh shakes his head.

"Something's come up, Bob. The woman who heads DevEx is here. I want to get to her before she leaves."

Bob's forehead is marred by a frown.

"That sounds important. What do we do now, Chan? I have just set up a con-call with Maarten, a financial journalist friend in Amsterdam. Apparently he told Priya he needs to speak to me pronto."

"You head to the hotel, Bob. Let me go and try to meet the lady. For all you know, it may not even happen!"

"Don't tell me she will turn down a meeting with the charming Chandresh Rajan?"

Chandresh gives Bob a droll look and asks the driver to drop him off at the main road.

CHAPTER 12

GANDHIPURA, 3 OCTOBER 2010

The receptionist at the hotel's front desk is fast asleep. Polite clearing of the throat and drumming of fingers on the desk have no effect on him.

Bob realizes that he can't afford to waste any more time observing social niceties. He opens his mouth to call out to the man when the telephone on the desk starts ringing loudly and he wakes up with a start. Mortified at having been caught napping, he is confused whether to answer the phone or attend to the "*gora*" guest. Bob cannot quite come to terms with the embarrassingly deferential, almost obsequious treatment that the colour of his skin merits in these parts. Chandresh often pulls his leg about it, feigning gratitude because he gets to bask in reflected glory.

Having decided to answer the phone first, the receptionist hurriedly ends the conversation and turns to Bob.

"Sorry, sir...sorry to wait you...any help?"

"Not a problem, but could you please help me? I need to connect to the internet and my connection is acting up.

103

Poor network. I was wondering if I could make use of the hotel's business centre."

The man looks at him in confusion.

"Business centre?"

"I mean the internet...the hotel's internet connection?"

The man looks at him mournfully.

"Very sorry...modem repair...mechanic no come!"

Bob has a sinking feeling in his stomach. Maarten must surely have emailed him the documents by now. How is he to access them?

Bob turns away and starts walking towards the elevator when the receptionist calls out to him.

"Sir, you try opening window?"

Bob is confused for a moment. Why would he try to open the window?

"Sir...window open...then maybe connection possible? Other peoples tries...work sometimes!"

Bob nods and smiles before getting into the elevator, hoping for one of those "sometimes".

He unlocks the door and walks into his room.

As he pulls the drapes apart, the bright sunlight filters in through the glass window panes. He switches off the air conditioning and opens the windows. A gust of hot air hits him in the face, reminding him of a ceiling fan that could still offer him some respite.

He pulls the table closer to the window and switches on his laptop.

Much to his own amusement, he mutters a prayer under his breath before trying to connect. The beliefs of the land seemed to be rubbing off on him too.

Maybe it is the window trick or just maybe, the Gods are pleased him after all!

Bob lets out a whoop of exultation when the connection goes through and he manages to log in.

The euphoria does not last long for he has no new mail.

Bob wonders what could possibly be keeping Maarten. It is quite unlike him to be so late. Maybe there had been another development that distracted him....

—–—

Bob had made the promised call to Maarten right after he had returned to his hotel room. The two had struck a good rapport when they had first met in 2009 as reporters covering the G-20 summit. Maarten was a senior correspondent with the BBC. Since then, they had often tapped each other for leads on stories that they happened to be working on or which might be of interest to the other.

Maarten had answered the phone almost immediately and came straight to the point without bothering with customary pleasantries.

"Bob, this must be the mother of all coincidences. I mean...I had called to get you to put me on to Chandresh Rajan and Priya tells me you are in India and with the man himself!"

Bob chuckled.

"Hello Maarten, I am good and hope you are too! So tell me, what do you want with Chandresh, if you don't mind my asking?"

Maarten barrelled on, ignoring Bob's not-so-subtle dig at the lack of a greeting.

"Bob, I need some information on microfinance institutions in India. I assume Chandresh will be able to help me with this?"

"What...are you working on a story on the microfinance sector?"

"Well, not exactly, I'm actually working on a story on pension funds. You know, how they are managing their investments given the economic meltdown and all that."

Bob's interest was piqued.

"Okay, is it that you notice a pattern with pension funds being invested in the microfinance sector in India?"

Maarten let out awhistle.

"Okay that was sharp, even for you!"

Bob let out a shout of laughter at the backhanded compliment.

"Actually, no. Just that I happen to be doing a story on the microfinance sector in India, obviously focusing on the international investment pouring into the sector, Wall Street being at the top of the list."

Maarten replied after an infinitesimal pause.

"Looks like my job is going to be a lot easier than I thought. So have you analysed the investment patterns, investor profiles...who are the big boys out there?"

"Well, it's the usual suspects. Most of the big venture capital funds are on the bandwagon: Lemoia, Alexander Zaimis—he has a big stake in at least two of the blue-chip MFIs—then there is the IT moghul, Jay Gupta, and of course the Indian IT giant, Raghav Shetty."

"Ever heard of Tejasvi Enterprises?"

Bob frowns.

"No, can't say the name rings a bell."

There was a pause.

"They are big players, with big money invested in two of the global giants among the MFIs—SAMMAAN Microfinance in India and Kapo in Nigeria. A few of our pension funds in turn have invested heavily in "Tejasvi.""

The mention of SAMMAAN set off warning bells in Bob's head. Could this possibly be a lead? What was Tejasvi and who were the people behind it?

He hadn't realized that he'd said it out loud until Maarten responded.

"I am trying to find out. All I know from a Google search is that the company was incorporated in Mauritius."

Bob chewed his lower lip as he tried to activate his tired brain cells.

"Mauritius...who can we tap there... Wait, I know! I have a contact there, a guy called Abdul. Let me call him and ask him to dig around a bit."

Maarten was excited.

"That's excellent! I knew I could count on you, my man!"

"Let us not get ahead of ourselves, Maarten. The lead may take us nowhere."

Bob struck a note of caution, if only to dampen his own rising excitement.

After promising to get in touch as soon as he got hold of some information, Bob ended the call.

He checked his watch. It was a quarter past one in the afternoon.

What was the time difference between India and Mauritius?

A quick Google search revealed that Mauritius was an hour and a half behind.

He suspected Abdul would be at work by now. Abdul ran a tourist agency in Mauritius and was extremely resourceful. Bob crossed his fingers and called him.

The phone was answered after a couple of rings.

"Hello Abdul, this is Bob from *The New York Post*. How are you?"

"Bob sir! How are you? It is so nice to hear from you after all this time...are you coming over?"

Not a bad idea. Maybe once he was done with the story, he could check with Priya if she could take some time off and join him in Mauritius. The idea appealed to him.

"Hopefully soon, Abdul, but right now I called to ask you for a favour."

"Anything, sir, Abdul is always at your service!"

"That is very kind of you, Abdul. I need information on a company called Tejasvi Enterprises, which was incorporated in Mauritius."

Abdul sounded hesitant.

"What kind of information? Are they doing illegal things?"

Bob hastened to clarify.

"Not really, at least not as far as I know. Just that they seem to have invested big money in the sector that I am doing a story on. I wanted to check out their background, their promoters, their line of business and so on."

"Okay, give me a few hours. Let me see how much I can find out and I'll call you back."

After hanging up, Bob tried calling Chandresh to check on his whereabouts, but there was no response.

Biting into an apple, Bob opened his laptop and started browsing through the DRHP (Draft Red Herring Prospectus) of SAMMAAN Microfinance that he had downloaded from their website. Next, he ran a search for "Tejasvi".

Sure enough, there it was!

On page 95, it said that Tejasvi Enterprises had bought a large number of shares, totalling up to nearly 15% of SAMMAAN's share capital. The DRHP suggested that Tejasvi Enterprises had bought the shares at par value during SAMMAAN's first round of institutional equity sales.

Bob was intrigued. An investor who was virtually unknown in the microfinance sector was part of the very first round of institutional equity sales. What made the MFI invite Tejasvi to partake in its equity sales? There had to be a connection there. Something didn't quite add up.

Tired of trying to solve the puzzle, Bob ended up dozing off on the chair.

The incessant ringing of his phone woke him up. His sleep-addled brain took a minute to process his whereabouts before he sat up with a start. The phone had stopped ringing by then, but he had grabbed it to check who had called. A cursory glance at the time revealed that he had been sleeping for more than an hour. He wondered if it was the heat that had brought on the spell of drowsiness. He had clean forgotten to shut the window and switch the AC back on.

The missed call was from Abdul. Did he have some information already?

With impatient fingers, he hit the call button.

It rang for a while before Abdul answered. He sounded a little out of breath.

"Sorry, sir, I was just making some lunch."

"I am sorry I did not take your call earlier, Abdul. I was actually sitting around waiting for you to call, and then I just fell asleep!"

Bob laughed.

"Must be the heat, sir.!"

"I guess so, Abdul. So, tell me, do you have news for me?"

"A bit, sir, not everything."

"I will need some more time to get details on the company's operations and interests, etc., but basically it is a venture capital fund. And the major stakeholder is a company called KPK Enterprises, based in Singapore."

Bob was intrigued. The trail seemed to be growing!

Taking his silence for disappointment, Abdul apologized profusely.

"I'm sorry I couldn't get you more information. Give me another day?"

Bob hastened to reassure him.

"Abdul, you've done a great job. This is a very important piece of information, thank you so much for your help. And please do let me know if you find out anything else."

After hanging up, Bob immediately dialled Maarten.

Maarten picked up after a few rings, his voice a mix of surprise and excitement.

"Don't tell me you have some news too!"

Bob grinned as he told him what he'd discovered.

"I don't know why, but I get the feeling that the trail

is headed somewhere big. We need to follow this one for sure. Do you have any sources in Singapore or should I employ mine? If something emerges I could even fly out to Singapore, it's a matter of four odd hours from here."

"But wait, tell me what you've got? Sorry, I got carried away in my excitement!"

He could almost hear the smile in Maarten's voice as he had responded.

"No sweat, Bob. The news I have is that Tejasvi just made an exit from SAMMAAN and made a killing in the process."

"What?"

"The news item just showed up while I was digging around. They've made huge profits. And there is pattern to it...they have already been down this road once...and come back through yet another QIP[6]...!"

Bob was stunned.

"You mean they had already sold out once before from SAMMAAN and then re-entered?"

"Exactly...let me read out a small piece from the report for you. I will, of course, mail you the entire piece along with some other material I have."

---

6 Qualified institutional placement (QIP) is a capital-raising tool, primarily used in India and other parts of South Asia, whereby a listed company can issue equity shares, fully and partly convertible debentures, or any securities other than warrants, which are convertible to equity shares to a qualified institutional buyer (QIB). Apart from preferential allotment, this is the only other speedy method of private placement whereby a listed company can issue shares or convertible securities to a select group of persons. QIP scores over other methods because the issuing firm does not have to undergo elaborate procedural requirements to raise this capital.

Bob listened intently as Maarten began to read.

"Interestingly, Tejasvi Securities Mauritius held 15% of SAMMAAN's shares up to August 2010 but exited the company during the first week of September as per shareholding data available on BSE. Tejasvi Securities then strangely re-entered SAMMAAN through yet another QIP offered at a lower price per share, at a very steep discount on the prevailing stock price. The QIP issue opened in the second week of September 2010 and closed five days later.... Tejasvi sold the stocks subsequently on October 1, making a huge profit of Rs 270 crores on the entire transaction."

"That is another huge killing!"

"So it appears, Bob...so it appears!"

"So what do we do next?"

"What do you think? Should we dig deeper? To be honest, this is not really the focus of my story."

Bob quickly interjected.

"Maarten, can I ask you for a favour? This whole thing has me thinking in a whole new direction. I'm going to scratch some more to get to the bottom of the holding company trail. And I might need your help with some of the legwork."

"Of course, Bob, I'd be glad to be of help. Maybe we could look at running a parallel story if something big comes out of it, you know, sort of like a joint operation!"

Bob smiled, thinking no journalist worth his salt would ever be guided by pure altruism when it came to a story that had the kind of ramifications as this one did.

A loud ping brings Bob back to the present.

It is the promised mail from Maarten.

Bob feels an all-too-familiar tingle at the back of his neck, a definite indication that he is on the verge of making an important breakthrough.

He quickly opens the mail and starts scanning through the documents Maarten has sent him. His instinct had not let him down after all. They were definitely onto something big here.

He suddenly has an epiphany and quickly glances at his watch. Singapore was just two and a half hours ahead of India. It must be late evening there.

He picks up his phone and dials Ron Whitefield, his colleague in Singapore, even as his mind continues to process all the information that he has received in the last few hours.

There is a long ring at the other end before the call goes through to Ron's voicemail.

Bob's lips curve in a faint smile as he listens to Ron, in his clipped British accent, request his caller to leave their name and number after a beep.

"Ron, this is Bob, Robert Bradlee from the New York bureau. Please call me the minute you hear this...top urgent!"

Bob slumps down into the couch, wondering idly if Lady Luck had favoured Chandresh too.

CHAPTER 13

Chandresh looks at the goon from the corner of his eye. Radhakrishna was supposedly part of the school administration. But his size makes Chandresh wonder if he hadn't been a boxer in a previous life.

He discreetly looks at his watch. It has been three hours since he was told to wait. He wonders if there is any point to it. Maybe he would be summarily dismissed in another hour or two?

"Do you have any idea when Ms Kumudini is likely to meet me?"

The Boxer gives him a baleful glance in response.

"Firstly, you do not have an appointment. Secondly, she has been kind enough to accept your request!"

Thirdly, shut up unless you want your face rearranged, Chandresh thinks to himself.

He pulls out his phone, thinking of calling Bob. But the phone network seems weak and anyway, there is not much he can tell Bob without Radhakrishna listening in.

He slips his phone back into his pocket and leans back in his chair.

Just then, the peon enters with a cup of tea.

For all his hostility, Radhakrishna has been a thoughtful host. This is the third cup of tea he has been served. A plate of assorted biscuits lies on the table next to him. Chandresh wonders idly if the hospitality is on Kumudini Potluri's orders.

Chandresh gives the peon a friendly smile, who seems about to respond but catches Radhakrishna's eye and scurries away after placing the cup noisily on the table.

Chandresh smiles determinedly at Radhakrishna and receives a glowering look in response.

Shrugging, Chandresh picks up the cup. The tea is particularly sweet, almost as if to make up for the company.

He had taken leave of Bob at the main road leading to the Gandhipura market more than five hours ago.

He had hailed the first auto that came his way.

"Padmavathi Nagar *pothara*?"

Thankfully, the driver agreed without any fuss—a pleasant change from his whimsical city-bred colleagues who were notorious for quoting exorbitant amounts.

The auto driver politely requested him to move towards his right to ensure balance. A tad puzzled, Chandresh nevertheless tried to comply and settled down on the middle of the seat.

During the bumpy ride through pot-holed streets, Chandresh wondered how to explain his sudden appearance to Kumudini and get her to agree to an interview. They were barely halfway when his reverie was broken by a huge thud.

The auto toppled to the left and came to a screeching halt. Chandresh was thrown to the side and hit his head against a rod. It took him some time to recover and compose himself. As he had stepped out, he saw that the left wheel had come off. Even while profusely apologizing, the auto driver pointed out that he had asked Chandresh to sit to the extreme right and not dead centre.

Still smarting from the blow to his head, Chandresh glared at him and handed him a twenty-rupee note before walking away.

Although Ramu had mentioned a landmark or two while scribbling down the school's address on a piece of paper, Chandresh kept getting lost and retracing his steps. It turned out that the auto had dropped him off at least a couple of kilometres away from his destination. As he plodded on in the oppressive heat, he realized he had no way of knowing if his quest was even going to yield any returns, but he couldn't possibly turn back.

Finally, he had come upon a half broken board that read Rajaji Nagar. Such was the joy he had felt on spotting the board that he had wondered idly if he would be happier standing at the pearly gates! Yet another passerby had given him directions to Sowjanya International School and kindly added that it was hardly a three minute walk from where they stood. Chandresh was hard pressed not to give him a hug out of sheer relief.

Finally, he stood before the massive gate that guarded the premises of Sowjanya International School. As he made to enter, his path was barred by a uniformed guard with a large moustache, an abrasive voice and a hand on his shoulder.

Chandresh mustered his most polite tone.

"Excuse me, I am here to meet..."

"No one is allowed to go in. The school is closed for two days."

Clearly, the management wanted to protect itself from nosy intruders.

Chandresh realized that he would never get into the compound if he were to reveal his true identity. One look at the high compound walls revealed that stealth wouldn't work either. So how to get past Mr Moustache?

After some quick thinking, he decided that aggression would be the best way forward.

"If you don't let me go in, you are bound to lose your job!"

That got him the man's attention. His composure cracked and an element of uncertainty crept into his body language.

"Listen, I am from the auditor's office. The income tax guys are coming again. I have some important papers here that I need to get to your boss before they arrive. If you don't let me in, I'll simply take them back. There will be a lot of trouble thereafter and your boss surely won't be happy to know that you were the cause!"

The man's face lost all colour and Chandresh knew his ploy had worked.

"Are you...sure...you're from the auditor's office?"

Chandresh assumed his most solemn expression as he reassured him.

The man seemed somewhat mollified. Then he opened the gate and waved Chandresh in.

The buildings seemed even more impressive from the inside. There were six buildings—three possibly housed the academic block, and three more at a distance, possibly the hostels. As he entered the centrally air-conditioned reception area, he was struck by the sheer opulence. The interiors were nothing less than what you would find in a similar institution in the metros or even abroad. A receptionist dressed in formal clothing manned the front desk.

He walked up to her and asked her if he could meet Kumudini Potluri.

She seemed surprised at the request, but tried to conceal it.

"She does not sit here. You will have to get in touch with her office in Hyderabad, please."

Her tone was courteous, yet firm.

"No ma'am, her office has asked me to meet her here!" he said as earnestly as he could.

"Are you sure, Mr...?"

"Ma'am, my name is Chandresh Rajan. This is to do with a story on the burgeoning growth of MFIs in India...it's for *The New York Post*."

He threw the last phrase in casually, knowing it would have the maximum impact.

Her eyes widened and her demeanour became a lot more friendly.

"Oh...I'm sorry! I was not informed that you were coming. Please have a seat? I'll just inform the administrator, Mr Radhakrishna. What would you like to have? Coffee, tea, or maybe something cold?"

Chandresh gave her his most charming smile.

"Thank you so much for your hospitality. I am fine, though, and looking forward to meeting Ms Potluri. And may I say what an international class institution you have here, Asha!"

The receptionist flushed with pleasure as she realized he had taken note of her name from the badge she wore.

"Ms Potluri must be very proud of the fine job you all are doing."

A shadow seemed to cross her face at that, possibly thinking back to the income tax raid.

She recovered quickly and smiled graciously.

"Ma'am is just wonderful. We are all in awe of her."

"Really? I'll make sure to quote you in the article!"

Her eyes widened at the thought. She gave him an extra sweet smile, which he returned without batting an eyelid.

She picked up the phone to alert her superior.

"Mr. Radhakrishna will join you in a few minutes. In the meantime, you must have a cup of coffee!"

"If you insist...please make that black without sugar, and maybe a couple of biscuits?"

"Of course, right away."

Chandresh picked up the magazine lying on the coffee table and browsed through it. It was a dated issue of a national news magazine but interestingly, it carried a glowing profile of Kumudini Potluri.

As Chandresh scanned through the article that was almost a litany in praise, he heard a deep voice bark at him.

He looked up to find a gigantic figure looming before him.

"Are you Chandresh Rajan?"

Chandresh merely blinked in response, before finally finding his tongue.

"Yes, I am..and you are...?"

"I am part of the Sowjanya administration. Why have you come here to meet Ms Potluri? This is not her office, and her office has denied asking you to meet her here."

Behind him, the receptionist looked at him with reproachful eyes but he blithely ignored her.

"Sir, my colleague, Bob and I have been repeatedly requesting an appointment with her for a story to be published in *The New York Post*, and we've been assured that we would be given time at the first opportunity. Since we heard that Madam Kumudini is here, we thought this just might be that opportunity. I would request you to please inform her that Chandresh Rajan is here to meet her. She knows me!"

"This is a school premises. You cannot walk in here to meet her on unrelated matters."

Chandresh gave him a hard look.

"I don't think it is all that unrelated. I believe she is here in connection with an investigation by the IT department. As a journalist, it is very important that I get to speak to her."

Radhakrishna's face darkened.

"That is a school-related issue. It has nothing to do with Madam Kumudini."

"Well, she must be concerned since your correspondent, Srinivas Potluri is her uncle!"

Radhakrishna glared at him for a few moments, then asked Chandresh to follow him.

He made Chandresh sit in his room and warned him that

he may have to wait long. It was also possible that he might not be able to meet Kumudini.

Chandresh assured him that he had nothing better to do with his time.

—◊◊◊—

After a further half hour wait, Kumudini Potluri deigns to make an appearance, striding into the room along with a couple of her assistants.

Of medium height and build, she exudes an aura of control. She is simply, yet tastefully dressed.

She lowers herself on the sofa across from Chandresh and waves the others away. Even the domineering Radhakrishna follows her instructions without demur, much like an obedient puppy.

"Yes, Chandresh, so what is it that couldn't wait until you were given a formal appointment?"

Seeing that she isn't going to waste time on pleasantries, Chandresh decides to take her cue.

"Madam, surely a response to the rising number of suicides on your watch cannot wait?"

"What do you mean on my watch? There have been four or five cases but they are the MFI's clients and that is about it. We don't control every aspect of their lives. I am sure you are aware of the growing suicide rate in the country as a whole!"

"There are eight documented cases and in every instance, the cause has been identified as inability to service the debts that have been piled on them!"

"I think that is an unfair criticism, Chandresh. We do not pile loans on to reluctant or unwilling clients. They exercise full and free will in every instance. And I repeat, there is no proof that they are debt-related suicides."

Chandresh wonders if she is simply trying to brazen it out or if she actually believes what she is saying.

"There is a definite pattern, Madam, and even you cannot be blind to it. What started out as a means to save lives is now taking them instead. There is a definite rot and there is no denying that."

Kumudini changes tack and speaks in a slightly softer tone.

"Well, what has happened is unfortunate and we are trying to see what we can do to help. In fact the insurance money has already been paid to the families and, of course, the loans have been written off."

"But I just visited Mylaram Kavala's family today and they claim that they have not received any settlement!"

Kumudini's face darkens.

"If that is true, I will ensure that the anomaly is addressed immediately and action is taken against the negligent staff."

"Madam, I am working on this story along with my colleague, Robert Bradlee of *The New York Post*. He is rather keen to meet you and, in fact that is why we have been bombarding your office with requests for an appointment. Anyway, the thing is, Bob has been keen to find out more about Wall Street investments in MFIs here. I'm sure you understand that this angle is of particular relevance to him. Don't you think it's interesting that the western capital markets are so keen to benefit from an industry primarily established to alleviate poverty in this country?"

Kumudini gives him a level look.

"Come on, Chandresh. Even you must admit that welfare models cannot sustain beyond a point. We need professionally managed self-sustaining business models that yield profits. What kind of lessons in enterprise management will we be teaching our clients if we are a loss making unit ourselves? And isn't it but natural for capital markets to be interested in profit-making enterprises?"

Chandresh gives her a half smile.

"I do not question your argument on self-sustaining models at all. However, given the very nature of the industry, the profit motive dominates the self-avowed motive of poverty alleviation and sustainable growth, to the point where MFIs are turning predators and devouring the very clients that they have sworn to serve!"

Kumudini shakes her head, and her lips curve in derisive amusement.

"Come on now, Chandresh. Aren't you being a tad melodramatic here?"

"Pardon me if I am. Maybe spending half a day under the very roof from which one of your clients hung herself has gotten to me."

Kumudini's face turns a deep red.

"Chandresh, I have a series of meetings lined up. So if we are done here...?"

"Madam, you'd have to agree with me when I say the objective of the sector is the financial inclusion of the poor and sustainable growth. But after the MFIs have converted to NBFCs, don't you think the poor have taken a backseat? I remember your statement around the time of creation of the MBTs[7] that it was to be wholly owned by your poor women clients. But your promoters and employees bought out their stake after hardly a couple of years at possibly a nominal value, and earned huge profits by selling out to foreign investment firms and venture capitalists."

Kumudini snaps at him.

"The inflow of commercial capital meant an expansion of our client base and their portfolios! How would you describe that as selling out?"

"It would be, wouldn't it, if the interests of your original clients—the ones who bore all the risk during the initial phase—are compromised in favour of the owners of the MFI and their employees?"

It is clear that Kumudini is losing her grip on her temper, but at this point, Chandresh is past caring.

"Madam, I must also tell you that we have found numerous irregularities on the ground. The records maintained at your branches are at variance with actual reality. There are several instances of ghost lending; some of the clients named in the records are either long dead or they do not even exist!"

Kumudini makes to get up.

"I will look into all these anomalies. Maybe you can share the specific instances with us?"

---

7 MBTs or Mutual Benefit Trusts are akin to private trusts and there is a lot of controversy surrounding their governance in microfinance in India.

"Surely your internal audit must have thrown up all of this?"

Kumudini folds her hands as a parting greeting.

"Of course, we will take care to correct all the wrongs that you have so kindly pointed out. Let me take your leave now."

Chandresh is on his feet too.

"Madam, one last request. Could I be allowed to a look into the financial records of the Sowjanya Group of Institutions?"

Kumudini frowns at him.

"Chandresh, I don't see how that has to do with anything. DevEx has nothing to do with this group. It just so happens that Srinivas Potluri is my uncle. And besides, the Income Tax raid was based on a wrongful complaint made by a detractor. The IT department has given them a clean chit!"

"That is wonderful, Madam. I don't see any reason why the records cannot be shared then?"

"Why should they be shared? This group has nothing to do with your story. And they are not obligated to share their records with whosoever wants to take a peek!"

Chandresh nods in assent.

"The group has nothing to do with the story...as long as there is no overlap between the finances of the group and those of DevEx?"

Kumudini loses her cool.

"I could sue you for defamation for accusing me of financial fraud without a shred of evidence!"

Chandresh shrugs.

"Following through leads and looking for evidence are

part of my job. You have no cause for concern as long as you are in the clear. Thank you so much for your time and patience, madam!"

Chandresh walks out of the room, closing the door on a furious Kumudini.

CHAPTER 14

The colonial-style bungalow in Lutyen's Delhi basks in the benign warmth of an autumn sun. It is that time of the year when the weather Gods are at their kindest towards the city's denizens. The pleasant nip in the air allows the society ladies to wrap themselves in Kanjeevaram silks and Pashmina shawls while the men strut around in nattily cut bandhgalas and Nehru jackets.

The flurry of flunkies and the red beacon cars outside the bungalow indicate that it belongs to someone in the higher echelons of government. The allotment of the bungalow had, in fact been a subject of bitter dispute, owing to both its location and the spacious grounds it stood on. Many a politician had wrangled for it before it fell to the lot of Nageshwara Reddy. Although not a senior member of the union cabinet, Nageshwara Garu wields great influence as leader of a regional party that is an important member of the ruling coalition.

Nageshwara Garu sits in his study, in deep discussion with

his secretary, Gopal Krishna and his political confidante, Suresh Babu. They are trying to chart out a strategy to handle a subject that is tabled to come up for discussion in Parliament later in the day. It has to do with the increasing number of debt-related suicides in Andhra Pradesh. Although he is a minister of state for environment, holding independent charge, he is one of the most vociferous MPs of the ruling coalition in Parliament. It would be incumbent on him to participate actively in the discussion, particularly since it is in the context of his native state.

"What is with our state and suicides? First the farmer suicides and now this. We must commission a study on why our people are so prone to taking their lives."

"Possibly because they are amongst the poorest and most exploited people in the country," Gopal Krishna thinks to himself, but is, of course, careful not to voice it.

"Annayya, you must highlight how our party has taken the district administration to task in Warangal and Ranga Reddy, with all those protest marches, etc."

"Suresh, in case you have forgotten, the party that governs our state is the very same party with whom we have since joined hands to form this national coalition. So we can't go into details of how we protested against them!"

Gopal Krishna intervenes.

"Sir, my informants tell me that the SAMMAAN issue will be raked up in particular. There have been more than 12 documented cases of suicide amongst their clients; and then the fire that destroyed numerous records at their office."

"My memory is excellent, thank you, Gopal Garu."

Gopal knows better than to respond.

"The member who has demanded a discussion on the topic, Rajendra...he claims to have toured five districts where there have been instances of MFI debt-related suicides. You must have seen the detailed report on his findings that he has tabled."

Nageshwara Garu closes his eyes and swears under his breath.

"I have. That chap is determined to settle past scores. All because we got his mining license revoked. It is a personal grudge, I know."

The door opens and a steward steps in.

"Sir, breakfast is laid. Madam has requested me to inform you that the guests are waiting."

"They are waiting to eat my head in parliament, and I am supposed to eat breakfast!"

The steward politely withdraws.

"Annayya, you need your strength to take those fellows on. Go and have breakfast. I will take my leave too. I'll meet you in the central hall at 10.30 sharp."

Gopal Krishna leaves.

Nageshwara Garu rests his forehead on his palms, gently kneading his temples as he tries to come up with a plan to counter the opposition charges. Meanwhile, his stomach rumbles in protest.

—⁓—

The array of dishes on display before Prasad Kamineni is no less than a spread fit for a king. There are the ubiquitous Indian dishes like idli, dosa, pongal, poori aloo, sambar and chutney, as well as traditional English breakfast fare including toast, porridge, an assortment of cakes, cereal, boiled eggs, pancakes and syrup, and a platter of fruit. It certainly looks more like a banquet one may expect to find at a five-star hotel than a home-cooked breakfast.

Krishnaveni Atha, his father's older sister, has always been extremely conscious of her status as erstwhile royalty. She married into an extremely wealthy industrialist family, and stood by her husband when he chose to enter politics. He had joined a national-level political party and was allotted a seat in the constituency that he was best suited to in terms of the caste mix of the voter population. As expected, he won by a landslide. However, because of internal party politics he was denied a party ticket the next time round. Smarting from the insult, he contested as a rebel candidate but lost by a small margin. Thereafter he formed his own regional party and contested the state assembly elections and managed to win a handful of seats. Buoyed by his success, he contested the parliamentary elections and won enough seats to emerge as an important member of the ruling coalition. His success had been attributed in part to a couple of matinee idols campaigning across the state on his behalf. The people of Andhra had always had a great fascination for film stars, whose support stood parties in good stead at the hustings. What the voters did not know was that the film stars supported Nageshwara Garu's party not because they subscribed to his ideology but because he was involved in financing their films, albeit always through an intermediary.

"Are you hungry, Chinna? We can get started if you like."

His aunt's voice breaks Prasad's thoughts. He shakes his head. That would defeat the whole purpose. He had been hoping to share his problems with his uncle over breakfast.

"Not really, Atha, let us wait for Mamaiyya. He must be caught up with some important work."

"You know how it is, Chinna, now that he is a minister, he hardly has time for anything other than work. The family is last on his list of priorities!"

Although it was supposed to be a complaint, Prasad could sense the pride in her voice. She was clearly enjoying holding court in Delhi as the wife of a central minister. No slouch when it came to fashion, now she looked even more the part with her silk saris in sober shades, an elegant string of pearls around her neck and a pashmina shawl draped over her shoulder. All the heavy gold jewellery was reserved for when she was back home amidst her own people, particularly in her maternal home where such simplicity would be found appalling. Privy purses and the concept of royalty may have been abolished but she remained their rajkumari or princess.

Prasad thinks back to his younger years, spent on his paternal grandfather's estate in their ancestral village. Thathaiyya had still been the overlord of several thousands of acres of agricultural land. They had lived regally in what was nothing short of a palace. They wore nothing but silk, used silver cutlery and had innumerable servants at their beck and call. His princely life had, however, been cut short in his early teens when he had to move to Delhi to live with his parents. Unlike his landlord grandfather, Prasad's father was an academician. An Oxford graduate in History and

131

Economics, he had taught in UK for many years before moving back to India and joining the Economics department at St Stephen's College. It was because of this that Prasad had spent many of his formative years with his grandfather.

His life underwent a sea change after the move. No longer the spoilt prince, he had to get used to attending to his own chores, although they did have some household help. His father had turned socialist in UK and lived the life that he preached. He actively participated in protest marches to highlight social causes and was associated with an NGO that worked in rural development. In an effort to shape Prasad's outlook, his father would take him along to several rural camps organized by the NGO. Although initially resentful about having to subsist on basics or less for even a few days, Prasad had slowly awakened to the reality that this was the life of the majority in this country. He often fancied himself akin to Prince Siddhartha, whose exposure to the harsh realities of life had made him renounce life and evolve into Gautama Buddha. His mindset went through even more of a change when he returned to his grandfather's home for the holidays. The poverty, oppression and lack of access to opportunities and resources that the villagers suffered from moved him to a point where he started experiencing a deep guilt for the excesses that he and his family enjoyed. He started feeling that the only way to assuage that guilt, even to a small degree, was to give back to the people who had been denied so much by his family over generations.

After graduating with a master's degree from Oxford University, Prasad briefly worked with an American investment firm. He had then surprised friends and family by giving it all up and moving back to India to work with an NGO called Madhya Bharath Vikas Sanstha. The SAMMAAN Microfinance programme assumed a new strategic direction in 1999, in the wake of the submission of his PhD dissertation on bottom of the pyramid strategies at the University of Michigan, Ann Arbor.

He put together a dedicated team of development professionals and spent a significant amount of time on the field during the growth phase of SAMMAAN. After studying various successful microfinance models across the world, like the Bangladeshi Nobel laureate, Mohammed Younus's Grameen Bank, he had come up with a model that imbibed the best of them all, while addressing the specific concerns of SAMMAAN's target clientele.

As a result of his personal standing and connections with Wall Street institutions, the apparent success of SAMMAAN's operations, as well as the media hype around them, SAMMAAN enjoyed significant support from the international financial markets. The company and Prasad's own growth thereafter had been dizzying.

Once the first flush of success abated, Prasad slowly began to realize that success was a double-edged sword. While more inflow of capital led to more growth, greater extension of credit and wider coverage, it also meant stiffer profit targets. The investors, while seemingly impressed with SAMMAAN's work in a sector intended to plug the gaps in financial inclusion for all, had been quite vocal in their expectations of high returns. Prasad found his situation akin to that of a man riding a tiger. Having accessed capital and extended his client base, he had to now necessarily continue to service their needs and achieve sufficient growth to offer attractive returns to his investors. After a point, in the quest to maintain a semblance of a healthy and growing portfolio and boost investor confidence, the targets had gone from stiff to ridiculous.

Once they started down the path of commercialization, Prasad felt that they were best off going the whole hog. An enterprise dedicated to bringing financial inclusion and ensuring sustainable growth had therefore evolved into a business operation that would stop at nothing in the pursuit of profits. Best practices fell by the wayside as they hurtled further down a path to no return.

Prasad had brought in a professional banker Venkatmurthy as CEO to accelerate the pace of institutional growth. And when Venkatmurthy had proved to be a stickler for adherence to set practices, a power struggle had followed. One that still remained unresolved and threatened to rock the foundations of the world that he, Prasad, had so painstakingly created.

While the reports on debt-driven suicides had merely disturbed the aura of complacency and self-righteousness around him, the fire at the SAMMAAN office had completely shaken Prasad. He had been genuinely fond of Sri and took the news of her death very hard. Privately, he blamed himself for the incident and felt extremely guilty, particularly in the presence of Sri's husband and infant son. It had been a wake-up call that roused him from a mindless quest for growth and a messiah-like sense of power.

How can a messiah admit that he has erred? How can he let the edifice that he has painstakingly built crumble?

How does he stand by and watch the uncovering of a sham that is partly of his own making? And how can he admit that he has gone horribly wrong, despite the best and most honourable of intentions?

The increased bustle in the room alerts Prasad to the fact that his uncle is about to join them for breakfast. He is almost thankful to be spared the strangling effect of his own thoughts.

"So...how are you, Prasad? Sorry I could not meet you last night. There was a meeting at the PMO."

Prasad jumps to touch his uncle's feet.

"Namaste Mamaiyya, I know you are extremely busy. I'm glad you had some time for breakfast with me."

Both of them know it is a meaningless charade that they are playing out for the benefit of Krishnaveni. The truth is, Prasad had arrived on the summons of his uncle. Nageshwara Garu knows that he has to have this talk with Prasad in their joint interest.

All conversation during the meal is centred on family gossip, with both men following Krishnaveni's lead. Prasad enquires after the welfare of his cousin, Supraja, who settled in the US after marrying a software engineer in the Silicon Valley. Nageshwara Garu talks with great pride about his son, Arjun, a graduate student at the Harvard Kennedy School of Government. It is his fond hope that Arjun will inherit his political legacy and take it to greater heights. The older son, Mahesh, handles their business interests in Visakhapatnam.

"Are you seeing Aarthi Shetty?"

Prasad is blindsided by his aunt's sudden query in the

middle of a discussion on the family's steel plant in Vizag. His personal life has always been a topic of speculation for the family, more so since his divorce. Given that his choice to marry Tracy Summers, who was American, had been a cause for lament within the family, one would have thought they'd welcome the divorce. But it ended up upsetting them even more since there hadn't been a single divorce in the family until then. So what if the couples were plain unhappy or even having extramarital affairs on the side. Prasad's decade-long marriage to Tracy had ended when she walked out on him two years earlier, taking their son, Udayan with her. He had often wondered if her disillusionment with the power broker that he had evolved into had been the cause of the breakup. Their relationship had, after all, stemmed from her deep admiration of his commitment to social transformation.

"Atha, what is this? Where did you get that idea?"

Krishnaveni gives him a knowing look.

"Although I live in Delhi, I have enough friends in Mumbai. I heard from a friend that you were with her at the success party of her latest film."

Prasad rushes to clarify.

"Atha, it is true that I was at the party, but I was not plastered to her side like your contact told you. I know the financier of the film. I happened to be in Mumbai and he invited me to it"

"I didn't know you hobnobbed with film folks too!"

Nageshwara Garu decides to end the conversation by dropping his napkin on the table and prepares to get up.

"Krishnaveni, will you please have coffee sent to the

study? Prasad and I have to catch up on some business matters. You'd get bored out of your mind."

Nageshwara Garu rises from the table and walks toward the door; Prasad follows him.

"I don't need to listen in, as long as you remember that Chinna is my favourite nephew—more like a son—and I want his interests protected at all costs!"

Krishnaveni's astuteness is not surprising, given that she has been married to a businessman-turned-politician for more than three decades. Besides, royal families are most often hotbeds of intrigue.

Nageshwara Garu gives her a curt nod and walks out of the room. Prasad gives his aunt a hug before quickly following him out.

Once they are settled in the study, and the bearer who brings them coffee leaves, Nageshwara Garu loses the final thread of patience that he has been holding on to.

"What the hell is going on, Prasad? How did you allow things to get to this point?"

Prasad feels like a child called into the headmaster's room for an explanation. He can't help feeling a little irritated by the unfairness of the situation, considering that in their case, the headmaster is almost as culpable as he.

"Mamaiyya, you know how it is. These things just happen all of a sudden, and the media just loves such stories."

"Didn't hear you complain about the media last year when you were hailed as one of the top influential personalities in the country's social sector!"

Prasad is mildly amused. His uncle is clearly not happy about the spotlight being on him.

"Mamaiyya, there is trouble brewing. And we need to find a way to get out of this mess."

Nageshwara Garu responds with an incredulous look.

"You tell me this when Rajendra Panisetty has tabled a motion in parliament to discuss this 'mess' as you call it! We are coalition partners with the party that is in power in Andhra Pradesh too, just in case you have forgotten."

Prasad runs his hand through his hair, beginning to feel tired.

"I am sorry, but, as you know, SAMMAAN is not the only MFI that is in a mess. The entire sector is in the midst of crisis."

"Possibly, but SAMMAAN is the largest of them all, and the only MFI with a huge public issue...and the only one that is headed by my nephew—which makes me directly answerable!"

Prasad lets out a heavy sigh.

"Mamaiyya, this is getting us nowhere. And more importantly, I have some bad news of my own. There is an internal crisis brewing...something that could blow up in our faces. Venkatmurthy is all set to stage a coup."

Nageshwara Garu's face darkens in anger.

"What are you talking about? How could you allow that to happen?"

Prasad's face turns deep red.

"I am sorry, it was a miscalculation on my part. He was giving us more trouble than support. But I really did not expect this kind of resistance from him."

Nageshwara Garu glares at him.

"Clearly timing is not your strength these days, as proven with the fire!"

Prasad looks stricken.

"Mamaiyya... that will remain the greatest regret of my life."

"Your regret is of no consequence, it changes nothing. What is the status of the investigations? I hope everything is being taken care of!"

Prasad merely nods. A sense of recrimination has clogged his throat. The intent, the consequence and then the cover ups—he is growing increasingly tired of it all. Would it be such a bad thing to let the tiger swallow him after all? He wonders if the clients who were driven to suicide had felt something similar.

"I cannot afford any scandal now, Prasad. There is talk of cabinet expansion, and I am pressing for a cabinet elevation. I've worked hard to get where I am, and I don't want anything spoiling it now."

Hasn't that been his story too? Not wanting anything to spoil all that he had achieved? In the heady pursuit of success and accomplishment, he allowed himself to be driven further and further way from the ideals that he had started out with.

"There is only so much I can do for you right now, whatever Krishnaveni may say. I also need to save my own reputation."

Prasad feels a surge of resentment.

"If SAMMAAN and I go down, a lot of other things will too. The loss will be all round...be it reputation or money. I am sure you don't want that happening, Mamaiyya."

Nageshwara Garu looks discomfited. His eyes dart around, as if to make sure they are not being overheard.

"I don't need your reminder, Prasad. I am quite aware of everything!"

Of course he would be, Prasad thinks to himself. Several hundred crores belonging to him and a few of his political colleagues had also been routed via SAMMAAN to several other businesses, including the film industry. It is surely in his interest to bail them all out!

Nageshwara Garu's phone rings.

"Hello, tell me, Jagadeesh?"

Prasad wonders if it is the party MLA from Warangal, Jagadeesh Eluru.

After a brief conversation, Nageshwara Garu thanks Jagadeesh for alerting him and ends the call. His face looks stormy.

"Prasad, when is your flight?"

"I'm taking the afternoon flight back, Mamaiyya."

"Postpone your return by a few days, and stay inside the house at all times!"

With that, he rushes out, leaving Prasad baffled.

CHAPTER 15

Badri Prakash, the constable taking phone calls at the Warangal Police Headquarters, is in a bad mood. He had requested a day off to visit his wife who was convalescing at her maternal home after giving birth to their first child last month. His superior officer, however, turned down his request on account of a political VIP's visit to the district. Badri's wife was very upset that he had not come to see her in over a week. So much so that she had refused to take his calls for the last two days. His mother-in-law informed him that she was suffering from postpartum depression. It hurt him that his wife did not believe that he was just as eager to spend time with her and the child.

The shrill ring of the telephone interrupts Badri's musings about ways to cheer up his wife. Disgruntled, he picks up the phone and mechanically reels out a greeting. It is an inspector from the Parichemam police station, asking to speak to the Superintendent of Police

141

of the district, Vishal Singh. Recalling that the SP is in a meeting and has asked for all calls to be put on hold, Badri informs the inspector of his unavailability. The inspector seems panicked and insists that he needs to speak to the SP immediately on an urgent matter. After some hesitation, Badri puts him through. The SP seems angry at the interruption; the inspector informs him that there has been a suicide in Parichemam village. The SP grumbles about how it has become a routine affair and asks him to collect data on which MFIs the woman is indebted to as well as the loan amount. The DM expects a report with all such information to be submitted to her office. The inspector hastens to clarify that it is not a debt-related suicide—ostensibly, at least. The man who has been found hanging from a tree on the outskirts of the village is a henchman of Bhava Reddy. There is a lot of unrest in the village and the inspector fears a law and order situation.

He is interrupted by some disturbance in the line and the call gets disconnected. Badri Prakash tries to call the inspector back, but to no avail. Meanwhile, commotion breaks out at the police station as the SP strides out of his office, followed by his subordinates. Badri Prakash immediately rises and salutes, even as he knows that the SP has probably not even registered his presence.

While walking out, SP Vishal Singh contemplates the possible law and order issues that could arise as a consequence of the incident.

—◦◦◦—

The police car races down the uneven village road, spraying mud in its wake.

Without waiting for the car to come to a complete halt, SP Vishal Singh jumps off and marches towards the spot where the cops from the local station have been trying their best to control the steadily swelling crowd. Vishal is surprised to see the numbers and wonders if the news has spread to the neighbouring villages too.

The local cops rush to salute him while the subordinates who have accompanied him try to clear a passage through the crowd for him.

After almost a decade of service, nothing much fazes Vishal. He takes in the sight of the man's body hanging from the banyan tree. The accompanying photographer starts clicking from different angles, while Vishal is briefed on the background of the dead man, Ramaiyya.

Unpopular in the village for being a drunkard and a bully who picked fights all the time, Ramaiyya's stars had been on the ascendant ever since he joined Bhava Reddy's band of men almost a decade ago. He slowly rose through the ranks and is said to have led several assignments over the last couple of years. He is survived by a wife and four children.

The body is slowly brought down. Vishal's sharp eyes don't fail to notice the matted hair above his temples, clotted with what looks like blood. There are also bruises on his arms and his shirt is torn in a few places.

A group of women start wailing loudly while beating their chests. When one of them tries to go towards the body, the cops hold her back. Ramaiyya's body is loaded on to a stretcher and carried to an ambulance.

As Vishal prepares to confer with the local inspector on the investigation, he is surprised to see a crowd squatting on the path to the ambulance, blocking its exit. A distraught woman argues with the cops, who try to persuade the crowd to clear the way. One of the cops points in his direction and the woman starts running towards him, while the rest of the crowd refuses to budge.

"Sir, she is Ramaiyya's wife."

Just as the local inspector warns Vishal, the woman cuts through the cordon around him and throws herself at his feet. Vishal moves back instantly while one of his subordinates barks out a harsh rebuke.

The woman starts weeping loudly, begging him for justice.

"Please stop crying, Amma. I understand you have suffered a loss, but you cannot obstruct police procedure. The corpse needs to be taken for a post-mortem."

Vishal appeals to the woman, hoping to make her see reason. But her weeping only gets louder.

"Sir, please don't cut my husband's body to pieces! Let him go in peace."

"Amma, the post-mortem has to be conducted if we are to determine the cause of his death."

At this, the woman stops sobbing and draws a deep breath before spitting out her words.

"You don't have to cut him to find out how he died. I will tell you...he was killed!"

"Amma, you cannot make wild allegations like that. We cannot conclude anything without proof. Only the post-mortem can reveal the actual cause of death."

The woman's eyes flash in anger.

"These are not wild allegations. It is nothing but the truth. Bhava Reddy killed my husband because he had become a liability. He was going to turn approver in the kidnapping case!"

Vishal looks at the local inspector for clarification.

"Sir, she is referring to the kidnapping of the minor girls that happened a few days ago. But there is no evidence of any sort..."

"The case that has to do with the SAMMAAN loan recovery agents?"

The inspector nods reluctantly.

"Sir, the parents had borrowed from other sources too. So we cannot confirm it was to do with SAMMAAN."

"Any evidence to prove that it had nothing to do with SAMMAAN?"

The inspector breaks into a sweat and shakes his head.

"No sir, no evidence."

Vishal turns to the woman.

"Amma, I think you are extremely distraught at the moment. Come and meet me at my office in a few days, after all the rituals are done. I promise you I will conduct a fair investigation and if there is evidence to prove your allegation, the guilty will be duly punished."

"Sir, a poor woman's good wishes will be with you if you ensure that justice is delivered. My husband has been murdered because he would have turned approver. I had promised DM Amma that he would give evidence!"

Vishal is surprised by this disclosure. *She knows DM Veena Mehra?*

"You've met the DM?"

The woman nods vigorously.

"Yes sir, a few nights ago, I went to her bungalow...you can ask her. She will vouch for me. Please help us, sir, I will give evidence in any court of law."

Vishal looks thoughtful as he assures her of his support.

———

Veena Mehra is in a meeting with the district block development officers, discussing the feasibility of implementing an international donor funded watershed programme over the next fourteen months. Her intercom buzzes, leaving her irritated; she had left specific instructions not to be disturbed. Although her PA Nilanjan knew her well enough to not bother her unless it was something very important.

She picks up the receiver and greets him brusquely.

"Madam, SP Vishal Kumar is here to meet you."

Veena frowns as she tries to recollect if they have a scheduled meeting or if she had summoned him on some count.

"Have we given him an appointment?"

"No, madam, but he says the matter is very urgent and cannot wait."

The creases on Veena's forehead deepen. What could have possibly happened for him to be so insistent?

"Please have him take a seat in the ante room, I will be there in a few minutes."

After replacing the receiver, she politely excuses herself for the next ten minutes.

As she enters the ante room, Vishal rises from his seat and salutes her smartly.

She nods in greeting and indicates for him to take his seat as she sits on the sofa across from him.

"Yes, Vishal, what was so important that you had to tear me away from my meeting?"

Without explanation or apology, Vishal gets straight to the point.

"Madam, do you know a woman from Parichemam village, Vijaya?"

Veena closes her eyes, trying to put a face to the name. A tear-stained face with imploring eyes, dishevelled hair and a thin frame wrapped in a faded synthetic sari come to mind.

"Of course, she barged into my bungalow a few nights ago, told me her husband was a henchman with Bhava Reddy."

"He was found hanging from a tree this morning, madam...a case of suicide, on the face of it. But I have my doubts."

Veena's eyes widen in shock.

"Vishal, she told me he was involved in the recent kidnapping case involving SAMMAAN and promised to get him to make a confessional statement, and begged for lenience in return."

Vishal sighs loudly.

"This is such a pity, madam. We have not been able to lay our hands on Bhava Reddy so far simply because there hasn't been strong enough evidence to seek his conviction. No one has been willing to testify against him."

Veena shakes her head.

"It is not just Bhava Reddy, it is also the powers behind him. Ramaiyya's testimony could have really helped, particularly in the SAMMAAN case. The crisis in the microfinance sector is proving to be a huge problem for the government—the suicides, the coercive debt recovery methods..."

Vishal nods in agreement.

"Things have been getting out of hand for a while now. Bhava Reddy's nephew, Chiranjeevi is backing SAMMAAN's coercive practices. His relative, Gopal Reddy works with SAMAAN."

"I think there is more to it than mere support, Vishal. There must be a transactional relationship of some sort. Bhava Reddy is no fool. And I won't be surprised if the trail extends beyond him."

"Ramaiyya would have been very useful, madam. He could have provided answers to a lot of questions—clearly why they did away with him!"

Veena looks at him sharply.

"Is that what you think it is?"

"I strongly suspect foul play. There were bruise marks on his body. We will have to wait for the post-mortem report, of course. The wife is convinced, though."

Veena considers his words.

"I think you should talk to her once she is more composed."

"I think she could be a possible witness; her inputs could help us in our investigation."

"I need to update MR on this."

Veena notices Vishal's puzzled look.

"The Principal Secretary, Maruti Rao. He heads the committee constituted by the CM to look into the crisis. He has instructed all the DMs to keep him constantly updated on any news related to the sector."

Just then, the door opens and Nilanjan enters.

"Madam, the Warangal District DM Subba Rao's PA is on the line. The DM wants to speak to you. I told them I would check with you and call back."

Veena frowns.

"Is there a pending issue with them, Nilanjan? Why are they suddenly calling?"

"No, madam, no pending issues that I know of."

"I'll take the call here. Put him through."

Nilanjan nods before leaving the room.

Veena looks at Vishal.

"Any Naxal-related issues?"

"I really doubt that, madam."

The phone rings.

Veena picks up the receiver and greets Subba Rao warmly.

"Hello Subba, hope all is well. I heard you wanted to speak to me?"

As she listens, her eyes widen.

"That is a big step! Have you discussed this with MR?"

Vishal wonders at the air of suppressed excitement about her. After a while, Veena finally ends the call and smiles broadly at Vishal.

"Subba Rao is getting an arrest warrant issued for Kumudini Potluri."

Vishal resists letting out a whistle.

"That is huge, Madam! I mean…Kumudini is extremely well connected. They would need some very hard evidence before making such a move."

"Apparently, someone related to one Mylaram Kavala has testified against DevEx. The accusations range from coercion to threats of sexual abuse, all of which allegedly contributed to Mylaram's suicide. And this information was brought to them by Chandresh Rajan."

"The journalist?"

"Yes, it seems he is collaborating with a journalist from *The New York Post* on a story on the Indian microfinance sector. He interviewed Mylaram's daughters and facilitated their meeting with the DM. There was an IT raid on a school that DevEx seems to have links with.

As Vishal processes the information, Veena continues speaking.

"Vishal, I want you to go to Parichemam. Meet Vijaya, ask her to talk to the family of the girls abducted by Ramaiyya. If they testify and we manage to dig up some dirt on SAMMAAN's links with Bhava Reddy, and the possible murder of Ramaiyya, I think we should be able to secure a warrant for the arrest of the SAMMAAN boss?"

Vishal's jaw drops.

"You mean Prasad Kamineni? He is really big fish, madam!"

Veena looks determined.

"All the more reason to get him. After all, nobody is above law!"

Vishal looks sceptical, but decides not to express his doubts.

"I will do my best, madam. That lady, Vijaya, will surely do her best to get us what we want, and if the evidence is strong enough, then we can move ahead with our plans."

Veena nods.

"I am going to discuss this again with Subba Rao. If we manage to bring in the head honchos, it will certainly provide the microfinance sector with a much needed shakeup!"

"True, madam. We still need to put together a collective body of evidence, cutting across districts, on their operations and tactics."

Veena looks thoughtful.

"Vishal, remember that woman standing next to Prasad Kamineni in that photograph that was plastered all across the press...where she is hitting the gong at BSE? I can't recall her name, but isn't she from our district?"

"Yes, though I don't remember her name either. But I do know another woman from the picture: Gangamma, one of the senior field workers at SAMMAAN. She is related to one of our drivers—I remember him bragging about her with the newspaper article. Should I find her?"

"Yes, it would be interesting to find out what happened to her after the stock issue. Meanwhile, I am going to call Chandresh Rajan. Let's try and set up a telephonic interview for him with this woman. It'll be good to get some media support on this. We need as many allies as we can get. Like you said, we are after big fish; so our net must also be stronger and spread wider!"

CHAPTER 16

Bob quickly scans his mail. The response is predictably defensive along with being a tad pompous in drawing attention to the bank's track record of exemplary commitment to equitable growth, financial inclusion and sustainable livelihoods for the poor and unbanked.

He picks up the cup of tea from the bedside table and sips from it absently. It is cold and flavourless; he wrinkles his nose in distaste, thinking fondly of the numerous cups of tea that he had consumed at roadside stalls, thanks to Chandresh. Tea had been their energy tonic and pretty much what kept them going as they travelled around the countryside to try and understand the causes of the rot that had set into the microfinance sector in Andhra Pradesh. Paperwork, account books, individual accounts, families, intermediaries—they had examined them all, and as they did so they were left feeling increasingly cynical about the growth story that had been bandied about in the media over the last many years.

He rubs his eyes tiredly and considers calling for a fresh pot of tea. He checks his watch and decides to put the thought on hold until Chandresh joins him. Chandresh had left to meet someone in the agriculture department regarding a fertiliser scam story that he was working on, promising to return in time for the scheduled Skype call with Maarten. Bob's colleague, Ron Whitewood had proved useful in tracking down information on KPK Enterprises, the Singapore-based firm that held majority stake in Tejasvi Enterprises. The firm's managing director was an Indian by the name of Kushal Prakash Rayudu. Bob was not too surprised to hear that KPK Enterprises was itself a subsidiary of KPK Ad Valorem, a company incorporated in Luxembourg. He already had a gut feeling that the trail was going to extend far; clearly, someone had gone out of their way to cover their tracks. Bob had passed on the information to Maarten, who agreed to continue further investigation. A day earlier, Maarten wrote to him, his tone a mix of mystery and suppressed excitement, and asked to schedule a Skype call, hinting that someone else might be joining the conversation.

Bob checks his watch yet again and realizes that there is still another hour to go before the scheduled call. He hopes Chandresh will make it. If Maarten's source proves useful, then Chandresh may be able to coax out more information from him. Just then, the doorbell rings and Bob hurries to answer.

"Hi, hope I am in time for the call?"

A harried looking Chandresh walks in and plonks himself down on the couch.

"Yes you are, I was beginning to wonder if you'd make it at all."

Bob walks over and takes the chair next to the couch.

Chandresh looks mildly irritated as he shrugs his shoulders.

"I wasted an hour waiting for an informant, who eventually proved useless!"

Bob calls room service and asks for a pot of tea along with some sandwiches.

Chandresh gives Bob a grateful look.

"So, have you heard from Ram Madhav?"

Bob's eyes twinkle.

"Just got done reading his response to the questions I had shot off. You were right, of course. It was the classic defence, along with impassioned declarations of commitment to the cause."

"Wasn't too hard to guess. I mean, what else would he say? That the banks spurred the MFIs on? And his bank, JBS, in particular, has the largest microfinance portfolio and they have been completely irresponsible and indiscriminate in pushing MFIs to keep lending without a thought to the absorption or repayment capacity of clients. Either there were multiple loans extended to the clients by the same MFI, or all of the MFIs split up the week amongst themselves to go and issue loans to the same clients. Why would the banks care as long as their targets are met? Or if a few clients have their lives snuffed out by the sheer burden of indebtedness. None of that shows up on financial statements anyway!"

Bob senses the deep bitterness in Chandresh's words, his disillusionment with an idea that had the potential to reshape the poverty paradigm. While he has known that things were not going quite right, he is taken aback by just how wrong it has all gone.

Their conversation is interrupted by the arrival of tea and sandwiches. Chandresh bites into the sandwich hungrily while Bob contents himself with a fresh cup of tea.

"By the way, I have a bit of interesting news. I got a call from the DM of Ranga Reddy district, Veena Mehra. She wants me to help them take the case against SAMMAAN further."

Bob waits for him to elaborate.

"Veena is one of the best IAS officers in Andhra Pradesh. She is particularly famous for the strong stand she took during an earlier microfinance crisis in the state in 2005. You might have read about it, we call it the Krishna crisis."

Bob nods.

"I think Subba Rao, the Warangal collector whom we met, has been in touch with her. Looks like they are working on a joint strategy to tackle the MFI bosses. There has been a spate of suicides in her district, and recently, the death of a potential witness who was to testify against the strong-arm tactics adopted by MFIs. They are trying to put together a strong case and she wants me to talk to the woman who became the face of the poor woman clients in the SAMMAAN IPO...you know, the woman who features in that historic photograph with Prasad Kamineni?"

"How will we track her down? Remember how the SAMMAAN staff fobbed us off when we asked them for her contact details?"

"The district SP is on the job. Veena wants me to talk

to the woman and see if there is any possibility that the investigation would benefit from some publicity...all of the MFI bosses have clout after all...so it would help to influence public opinion! Besides, I would really like to know what difference this whole IPO has made to her life. And what she thinks of the suicides that have followed." Bob looks thoughtful as he nods and adds, "I get where she and you are coming from."

He then checks his watch again and exclaims.

"Oh, it's time."

While Bob calls Maarten, Chandresh tries to tidy up.

Maarten greets Bob with great cheer.

"Bob, I was beginning to wonder if you had forgotten. Tomas here is a busy man!"

Bob apologizes and introduces Chandresh.

"Maarten, Chandresh and I go a long way back, just like you and me. And obviously, given that we're on his home turf, you could say he is the boss on this one!"

Chandresh laughs.

"Maarten, Bob is just being polite. But let me tell you that I have followed some of your stories and it's a pleasure connecting with you."

"Likewise, Chandresh. Now, let me tell you more about Tomas, the star of the hour. Tomas Lindquivist, gentlemen, is something of an expert on the subject of money laundering and the international trafficking of money."

Bob and Chandresh exchange glances. *Where is this conversation going?*

"We are in Tomas's home in Brussels. I flew in this morning, and we have had a rather enlightening conversation."

Where Angels Prey

Bob is intrigued. If Maarten took time off his busy schedule at the BBC studios in London to fly to Brussels, there must be a very good reason.

Maarten continues, "Tomas used to be part of the European Union core group that framed the anti-money laundering legislations. He's been retired for some time now, but he's still the go-to guy for several agencies because of his well-known expertise in unearthing *hawala* transactions. What really made him famous, though, was when he managed to crack the Al Qaeda's methods of transferring monies across continents and discovered how they shared information on such transfers. He was the first to reveal how they operated several email accounts but never sent a message about the money transfer. You see, the same account was accessed by various operatives across the globe and they would communicate with one another by typing messages and saving them in the Drafts folder. So no e-mail had to be sent. This simple but effective trick had kept the international investigators at bay for a long time before Tomas Lindvquist miraculously cracked it."

Bob and Chandresh are, of course, suitably impressed by Lindvquist's exploits but are also impatient to know how all that could be relevant to the Tejasvi Enterprises trail. Maarten, meanwhile, rambles on about another case that he has worked on closely alongside Tomas.

Bob decides to steer him back.

"Wow, this is all just amazing. In fact I think *The New York Post* would be very interested in profiling Tomas. We could do an in-depth interview...but, getting back to the issue at hand, Tomas, do you have any hunches on Tejasvi?"

157

"Hello Bob and Chandresh, pleasure to connect with you guys. I'm glad to be of some help. As for Tejasvi, the trail extends from Luxembourg to the US. The holding company, Tejasvi Imports, is incorporated in the US, in California to be more precise."

"Oh really! I assumed from the name that it wasn't an investment firm. What does the company import? And who are the principal investors?"

"No, it is not an investment firm, really. While they seem to have an import license for Indian spices, I don't see them actually importing very much...unless you count money—there are huge money transfers taking place at regular intervals. And the majority stakeholder is a man called Pradeep Vangal—does the name ring a bell?"

Bob looks at Chandresh, who indicates that he has no clue.

Tomas watches this silent exchange.

"One other thing—much of the money is coming in from India, from Hyderabad to be particular."

"Vangal is a common surname among the Reddy community, so I can get the Hyderabad connection, but it does seem like an incredibly roundabout way, don't you think? Crisscrossing through three continents to invest in your own backyard?"

Tomas nods in agreement before offering his own take.

"Well, not so roundabout if the idea is to cover your tracks. See, it took us three days to get to the source, or almost three days, and that too because we were looking."

Chandresh nods his head thoughtfully.

"I agree, and the fact that the company has no apparent

connections to the microfinance sector, not even as an investment firm, makes you wonder how and why the interest in the sector. What do they even know of it? And what is it that makes them invest in MFIs across the world?"

Bob nods.

"That is indeed key—their inordinate interest in the sector that has nothing to do with their stated line of business and, of course, the Hyderabad connection. I would like to track the inflows back to their source, see if there is any connection with any of the big bosses back here."

Chandresh doffs an imaginary hat to Bob.

"Excellent, that is exactly what we must do now!"

Maarten and Tomas smile.

"So Bob, Tomas will be sending me some documents on this that he has managed to collect. I will share them with you, of course. Do keep me posted on the news at your end. This is turning out to be a cracking story—Wall Street and European pension funds making huge profits out of lending to the Indian poor!"

After the Skype conversation comes to an end, Chandresh turns to Bob.

"So, did Prasad Kamineni's office get back with a time?"

"It seems he's not in town. His office claims they don't know when he will be back."

Chandresh raises his eyebrows.

"That is surely strange. But Prasad's PR skills are impeccable...even when he knows you are not going to write a puff piece!"

Bob looks thoughtful.

Ramesh S Arunachalam

"I wonder if it has anything to do with the proposed action that you mentioned earlier."

Chandresh ponders over Bob's words.

"It's possible. Maybe he got wind of something? Not surprising considering his connections in high places. You know his uncle is a union minister, right?"

"Good for Prasad. Chan, we need to track down this Vangal chap. How are we going to do this?"

Chandresh thinks for a minute before responding.

"Ask Google maybe?"

Bob half snorts.

"Things can't be that simple!"

"Sometimes they are. The answer is right under our nose, just where we are sure not to look."

Chandresh runs a search on his laptop.

When Google does not yield much, he signs into his Facebook account to continue the search. They come across two Pradeep Vangals in the Silicon Valley, one of whom has three common friends with Chandresh. After checking the time, Chandresh calls one of them. He informs Bob that she is his cousin.

There is no response at the other end. Just when Chandresh is ready to hang up, the call is answered.

Chandresh puts the phone on speaker, and Bob can hear a disgruntled, sleep slurred voice snap at Chandresh.

"Chandrunna, there is such a thing as time difference, you know!"

Chandresh is not perturbed in the least.

"Sowmi, this Pradeep Vangal—he is on your FB friend list—who is he?"

160

The response at the other end is a snort.

"Are you kidding me? You woke me up at 4 a.m. for this?"

"Listen, Sowmi, this is very important. Just tell me who he is. Does he run an import-export business?"

"Not that I know of. He is a techie."

Chandresh is somewhat disappointed.

"Are you sure? How well do you know him? Do you have his address?"

"He lives two streets away, and I know him reasonably well. He definitely doesn't run a business. His family has a restaurant though. They have been living in the Valley for the last 30 years."

Chandresh sighs heavily.

"Okay, Sowmi, sorry to have disturbed you. He is probably not the guy we are looking for."

Just as he is about to end the call, Sowmi adds...

"Don't know about that, but you may know his family. His wife, Supraja is the daughter of that politician, Nageshwara Reddy. I think he is a union minister now, right?"

Chandresh pumps his fist in the air as he thanks his cousin profusely for the tip off before ending the call.

"Have we made a breakthrough or what! Pradeep is married to Nageshwara Reddy's daughter, the man who is Prasad Kamineni's uncle and chief benefactor!"

Bob displays a more cautious enthusiasm.

"I guess we could be onto something here, but prima facie, all we know is that a certain Pradeep Vangal is the son-in-law of a senior Indian politician, who is also the uncle of one of India's microfinance messiahs."

"Are you serious, Bob? Do you actually believe this is

nothing more than a coincidence? That this Pradeep Vangal has nothing to do with Tejasvi or Prasad, or that Prasad Kamineni is not in fact trading in the shares of his own company? Insider trading, damn it! That is what this is called."

Bob looks at him calmly.

"Chan, I am not disputing all that you say. It could all well be true, but what physical proof do we have to nail this? We are only speculating here!"

Chandresh's eyes flash in anger.

"Okay, so we don't have hard proof yet. But I'm sure your gut—the famous journalist's gut—says the same thing that mine does, which is that Prasad has his hand in the cookie jar. In fact, I'd say he's in it right up to the elbow. As for evidence, we *will* find it. I am not letting this guy get away, Bob. The fraud and deceit lurking behind the veneer of sincerity and commitment...he will have no place to hide before I am done with him!"

Bob sighs.

"All of that sounds great, but how are we going to do this? Where do we begin?"

Chandresh's phone rings. He looks surprised and then puzzled as he looks at the screen, then quickly takes the call.

Bob can sense the underlying excitement in his voice while Chandresh tries to sound calm and courteous. He ends the call after agreeing to meet the caller the next evening at the Kakatiya Sheraton hotel.

As he turns to face Bob, Chandresh's expression is a mix of anticipation and pure glee.

"Would you believe it? There we were, breaking our

heads over evidence, and here the evidence practically knocks at our door!"

Bob looks at him quizzically.

"That call was from Venkatmurthy, erstwhile CEO of SAMMAAN. He wants to share confidential information with us, on the various misdeeds of Prasad Kamineni!"

Bob looks startled.

"Venkatmurthy is no longer CEO?"

"Apparently not, although the news is not public yet. Clearly he must have locked horns with Prasad...and now he is determined to get his pound of flesh!"

Chandresh smiles broadly.

"We have just had a massive stroke of luck, Mr Westwood. Let me take you to Paradise for a treat!"

Seeing Bob's puzzled expression, Chandresh starts laughing.

"The shop that serves the best biryani in Hyderabad if not the world!"

CHAPTER 17

PARVATHAPURAM (RANGA REDDY DISTRICT),
7 OCTOBER 2010

The sky is overcast. Renuka walks down the narrow path that leads to her village as quickly as she can without disturbing her head load of firewood. Every day, she traverses the five-kilometre distance from her village to the nearby forest in order to collect firewood for fuel. She takes yet another peek at the skies, hoping the rain Gods will have mercy on her. Damp firewood would leave her with no means to cook for her family the next day. She wonders if her husband has remembered to milk the cows. The milk collections agents hate to be kept waiting and she can't afford to displease them.

Lost in thought, Renuka almost bumps into the teenager running towards her.

"Pinni! Please run and hide...the police are after you!"

The boy, Ramu, is her neighbour, Champa's son. He has a reputation for being a prankster.

"Go away, Ramu, I have no time for your pranks today. I need to get home before it starts pouring!"

Ramu shakes his head vigorously.

"Pinni, it is not a prank. There is a police jeep and a red beacon car. The cops are looking for you, I swear!"

Renuka is genuinely afraid. Why were the cops looking for her? What had she done? Where could she run and hide? How long could she hide anyway?

Just then, she spots her husband, Krishnaiah cycling towards her. *What was going on?*

"Renuka...run quick! They are waiting for you; go as fast as you can!"

He grabs the load of firewood from her head and gives her a gentle push.

"What is happening? Who is waiting?"

"DM Amma is waiting, you idiot. She is sitting inside our house and she wants to meet you. Run along! I will go to the kirana shop on the main road and get some cold drinks."

Krishnaiah hands over the firewood to Ramu and cycles off.

Renuka runs down the path leading to the village. *Surely they would not arrest her if DM Amma was their guest?*

A bevy of cops stand at the entrance to the lane leading to Renuka's house. Two jeeps and a car are parked nearby.

Seeing her approach, one of the cops calls out to her.

"Hey, are you Renuka?"

She nods fearfully, her mouth dry from all the running and the fear that the uniform and baton automatically evokes.

"Go in quickly, DM Amma and SP Ayya are waiting for you."

She quickly nods, mops the sweat off her face with the

end of her sari, and enters the house. She is astounded by the sight that greets her.

DM Veena Mehra sits on the best (and only) chair in the house, with SP Vishal Singh standing beside her. But that isn't what has Renuka taken aback. What astounds her is what the DM is doing—reciting a nursery rhyme along with Renuka's youngest daughter, four-year-old Subbulakshmi, who goes to kindergarten.

The girl spots Renuka and promptly rushes to her side, hugging her legs. Renuka's older daughters, Gajalakshmi and Varalakshmi, remain seated where they are, by the side of the DM, with their books spread around them.

"Your daughters are very bright, Renuka. I'm impressed!"

Renuka beams shyly before looking fearfully at the SP.

"Don't worry, Renuka, this is just a casual visit. You have nothing to worry about. And SP Vishal Singh is not an ogre; he won't eat you up!"

Renuka is embarrassed and remains silent.

"I know your name. Do you know mine?"

Before Renuka can answer, one of her daughters pipes up. "DM Amma!"

Veena laughs and pats the child on the head.

"That is not my name, silly. My name is Veena...Veena Mehra."

Renuka's lips try to form the name silently.

"So, Renuka, I belive you are a very famous lady!"

Renuka looks at her in confusion.

"I mean, didn't you have your picture come out in the newspapers? Along with your—what's his name—Prasad Kamineni?"

Renuka shakes her head and corrects her.

"Annaiyya!"

"Yes of course, Annaiyya. So how did you like the trip to Mumbai?"

Renuka answers her shyly.

"It was nice, so much bigger than our village! But I missed my family...and my cows."

Veena and the SP exchange smiles.

"Yes, of course, nothing like home. Tell me, Renuka, why exactly did you go to Mumbai?"

"Bomakka took us. She said there was some meeting. We go sometimes when there are meetings and some big officers come."

Veena nods. Vishal shoots a question at her in a stern voice.

"It was not just a meeting, was it? Did you know that the company that you hold shares of is a listed company that is worth hundreds of crores?"

Renuka looks at him blankly. Veena gives her a reassuring look.

"I don't know about all that. Bomakka just told us that it was some meeting..."

"That is fine, Renuka. So tell me, have you been paid any money since the Mumbai meeting?"

Renuka shakes her head in vehement denial.

"I have three more instalments to repay on my current loan. Maybe I will get another loan after that."

"What about the others? Have you taken loans from the others? DevEx, Aashray...?"

"I repaid another loan six months ago. That was DevEx—

it was for building a cow shed. The SAMMAAN loan was to buy a cow."

Just then, a cop enters the house with Bommakka in tow.

Bommakka, terrified to see the DM and the stern looking SP, dives straight to the DM 's feet and prostrates herself in supplication.

"Amma, I have not done anything wrong, please don't send me to jail!"

Veena asks her to get up and assures her that she is not going to be arrested.

"Bommakka, Renuka was just telling us about the Mumbai meeting. What do you remember of it?"

Bommakka gulps before answering in a small voice.

"Amma, I was just asked to identify three or four members from our district to be taken to the meeting. The elders and the men of the village were not happy, but the office people, Nagalakshmi Akka, said everyone will be safe. She also said something about how we were all owners of the new company...how all of us would benefit..."

"But Renuka says she has not got any money after that meeting. So what is this about being owners of the company?"

Vishal adopts the same stern tone that he had used with Renuka and asks about the company and the shares they hold in it. The otherwise bold Bommakka is petrified and answers him between sobs.

"Ayya...I don't know...even I haven't got any money. When my niece got married, I desperately needed more money, so I went to Hyderabad to meet Nagalakshmi Akka, but she said I already had two running loans and that she wouldn't give me any more. I asked her why she had told us we owned the company. She got very angry and shouted at me. I had no choice but to go to a private moneylender. But he shouted at me too, saying that I had ruined his business by taking all the women to SAMMAAN. It was a very difficult time."

Veena tries to comfort her.

"Okay, Bommakka, stop crying now. Tell me, what about all these instances of suicide? Eight people have committed suicide so far in our district, including that fellow, Ramaiyya of Parichemam village. Are you aware of these things?"

Bommakka nods her head as she responds in a small voice.

"Amma, one of them is my son-in-law's aunt. We have all been very upset. But we have accepted it as our fate. Nagalakshmi Akka told me that it is all because of our greed. We took too many loans and now we are killing ourselves because we cannot repay them."

Veena's eyes flash in anger.

"So why did all of them issue concurrent loans in the first place? Did you not tell them you had already taken loans from others?"

Bommakka shakes her head.

"No, Amma. In our village, we have a weekly schedule. SAMMAAN agents come on Monday, DevEx on Wednesday, and Aashray on Thursday. They decided on this in consultation with each other. Often they even use the same collection agents."

Vishal turns to her.

"And have they ever threatened you, or anyone else? Coerced or forced you in any way to repay your debts?"

Renuka's eyes instantly fill up with tears.

"Sir, once I could not pay my instalment on time. I had to pay my children's school fees. The agents...three men... they came and sat in front of my house and refused to leave. They'd say horrible things to me each time I left the house. My neighbour got very angry with me because a boy's family was coming to see her daughter the next day and she said it would look very bad if they saw men sitting around like that. So I borrowed the pending amount from my aunt who lives in the next village and repaid them the next day. Only then did the men leave. I felt so ashamed..."

Tears roll down her cheeks as she recalls the humiliation.

At this, Bommakka pipes in.

"Ayya...my relative...she had a daughter...the girl was to be married soon. But she didn't repay two successive instalments and the agents went to her house and started abusing her publicly. They spoke ill of her family and her character, and because of that, the marriage was cancelled. The girl was heartbroken, and my relative could not bear the shame, so she committed suicide...because she blamed herself for what had happened."

Bommakka sighs before continuing.

"They had also taken loans for the wedding....and had already spent a lot of that money. She knew she was going to default on the loans, so she thought she would kill herself and maybe that way her family would be spared."

There is a long silence, before Bommakka speaks again, this time in a low voice.

"I was the one who got her into SAMMAAN. Sometimes I feel like I killed her myself."

Her mumbled words pierce through the thick silence in the room.

"Bommakka, trust me when I say this—if they say you were greedy for taking multiple loans, they are far greedier. They issued loans to you without giving any thought to your capacity to repay. And then resorting to coercion to get you to pay money that you simply don't have! For all their talk of altruism, they have behaved worse than loan sharks. They exploited your weakness and, in the process, made far more money than you can even dream of. ...We have to do something about this, and you need to stand with us—all of you. Without your voice, we will be helpless!"

A short silence ensues although the weight of Veena's impassioned plea hangs heavy in the air. The ringing of Vishal's phone breaks the silence. He seeks Veena's permission to take the call.

His conversation ends in just a few seconds, after which he turns to Veena and says in an undertone.

"Ramaiyya's post-mortem report has come in. The cause of death has been established as asphyxiation...but it also says that the bruises on his body indicate extreme physical torture."

Chapter 18

Veena looks at the piece of paper in her hands. She cannot resist feeling victorious. It took a lot of hard work but they eventually managed it!

It was not often that "icons" get taken into custody. Named among the most influential minds in the country, féted by the international and national media alike...yet no one is above the law of the land.

She hands over the arrest warrant to a beaming Vishal.

"All the best, Vishal!"

"Thank you, madam, but for your initiative this would not have happened."

"We owe it to them—to each of those fifty plus people who have been robbed of their lives, and to the hundreds of thousands of others whose trust has been violated."

Vishal nods before taking her outstretched hand in a firm grip.

"I will take your leave now. We want to be in Hyderabad before noon."

He salutes her smartly and strides out of the room.

Veena wonders how Prasad Kamineni will react when he is served with an arrest warrant. She recalls her first meeting with him almost a decade earlier, when both of them had been honoured for their achievements by a citizen's forum. He had come across as a smooth and charming man, keen to impress her with his vision for financial and social inclusion of the poor. Yet she had been left with a vague feeling of disquiet. After the Krishna crisis, she had begun to question some of the microfinance models that were in place. While their avowed aim was to release the poor from the clutches of usurious money-lenders, many MFIs themselves charged interest rates that were no less exploitative. Moreover, their coercive tactics and blatant flouting of established norms, coupled with the absence of any proper monitoring mechanism had made them even more dangerous than informal moneylenders. The blatant commercialization of the microfinance sector over the last five or six years had only aggravated the existing lacunae in the models.

Subba Rao had also secured an arrest warrant for Kumudini and a police team was on its way from Warangal to apprehend her. Veena hopes the double strike will have a significant impact on the working of the sector. The case of Mylaram Kavala had received state-wide attention; even a national television channel interviewed her hapless daughters as part of a news report on debt-related suicides in the state.

Veena cannot but help feel grateful to Vijaya as well.

173

Despite her personal tragedy, she had worked hard to convince the family of the girl abducted from the village to testify against SAMMAAN. Although they did not yet have enough evidence to act against her husband's killers, she had kept her side of the bargain. And despite the fact that her husband had been one of the abductors, his death erased any hatred or ill will the family bore towards him. Strangely, they even sympathised with him, possibly because of the goodwill Vijaya herself enjoyed. Whatever their reasoning, they had helped strengthen the case against SAMMAAN. Their testimony, along with those of Bommakka, Renuka and a few others, had meant that a strong case of financial fraud, criminal intimidation and kidnapping could be built against SAMMAAN and Prasad Kamineni, its founder-promoter.

While the police had managed to interrogate Bhava Reddy's nephew, Chiranjeevi, on the Ramaiyya murder case, they had no strong evidence to proceed against him and his cohorts. They were yet to establish Bhava Reddy's support to the debt-recovery operations of SAMMAAN and other MFIs. While a few underlings had been rounded up for questioning, there was no breakthrough yet. Veena hopes that they will be able to persuade at least one of the men to testify to the politician's association with SAMMAAN, and Ramaiyya's murder in particular.

Feeling satisfied, even if momentarily, Veena goes back to her desk, where a large pile of files awaits her attention. She has hardly begun work when her mobile phone rings. Veena's face brightens as she sees that the call is from MR.

"Good morning, sir, are you back? I called your office the

day before since your phone wasn't reachable. They told me you were in Delhi. I needed to talk to you about something important..."

"I wish you had, Veena. Then maybe both of us could have been spared this embarrassing conversation."

Veena feels deflated.

"I'm sorry sir, is there an issue?"

She hears a heavy sigh at the other end.

"What is this joint operation with Subba Rao?"

"Sir, I already mentioned to you that we are collaborating on the issue, since our districts are the worst affected."

"You told me you were working together to build a strong case, not that you were sending men out to arrest Prasad and Kumudini!"

"Sir, isn't that the logical conclusion? Given the rising death count and charges of financial fraud and coercion, the move against the head honchos of the MFIs was but inevitable!"

"I wish you had consulted me before issuing the warrant, Veena. I would have saved you the trouble."

"Sir, I am confused..."

"I have just spoken to Subba Rao and given him the same instructions—call your men back, Veena. Prasad and Kumudini are above the law and cannot be touched."

CHAPTER 19

"The presence of globally recognized microfinance players like SAMMAAN has, of course, contributed significantly to the success of the financial inclusion campaign in the state."

The completely unintended irony in the statement does not escape Chief Minister Sudhakar Reddy. As of last count, the said success has claimed close to sixty lives. He wonders if Thomas Warner, the $400-a-day development consultant deputed by the international donor, knows this.

The meeting in progress at the CM's chambers is on the Universal Financial Inclusion Project, an international donor funded initiative implemented in collaboration with an apex development bank in India. After a pilot phase in three districts in Tamil Nadu and Maharashtra, they seek to expand to Andhra Pradesh and Karnataka. Besides Thomas Warner, there is his Indian counterpart, Rajesh Sharma, who probably gets paid half of what the American consultant does. Maybe in deference to that, he lets Warner do most of the talking. Principal Secretary Maruti Rao waits for the consultants to go through their pitch before offering his comments.

While Warner continues to highlight the Andhra Pradesh success story, the chief minister wonders how he should break it to them that they are planning to pull the plug on it. Ever since coalition politics has caused him to put a halt to the legal proceedings against the MFI top bosses, Sudhakar Reddy has been smarting. He has had to go through the ignominy of requesting MR to put on hold proceedings that he himself had authorized.

"Mr Warner, the state administration is trying to resolve some issues that have cropped up at the ground level, issues that you may have encountered yourself during your field visits. We will study in detail the approach paper that you have so kindly shared with us, so we can arrive at an understanding on the ways forward."

The chief minister gathers his meandering thoughts as Maruti Rao smoothly brings the meeting to a close. Even as the consultants take their leave after a round of polite handshakes, the CM's PA, Lokesh steps in with a rather harried expression.

"Sir, you are scheduled to meet the representatives of the employees' union after lunch. But the collectors of Warangal and Ranga Reddy districts are already here, along with the CEO of TERP, Mr Rashid. They say it is imperative that they meet you at the earliest."

Sudhakar Reddy looks at the Principal Secretary questioningly but the latter seems equally unaware. After instructing his PA to send in the bureaucrats right away, the chief minister sips from the fresh cup of coffee that has just been placed on his desk. It is close to lunch hour but obviously this meeting must take precedence over all else.

All three bureaucrats have almost identical expressions at this point—a mix of tension and nervous excitement. They greet the chief minister and principal secretary with due deference before Rashid takes the lead and apologizes for requesting a meeting without prior notice. "When Subba Rao Garu met me at my office earlier and shared the information with me, I thought it important to apprise you of things at the earliest," he offers in explanation.

"I assume this has something to do with the microfinance sector?"

Maruti Rao's question is more an observation, since the presence of Subba Rao and Veena Mehra is a clear pointer in that direction.

"Yes sir, it appears that Prasad Kamineni and company are not going to be spared after all!"

The chief minister looks closely at Veena Mehra as if to detect any hint of underlying sarcasm, but her face is wiped clean of any expression. He wonders if it is his imagination after all, prompted by the sense of failure that he has been grappling with.

Meanwhile, Maruti Rao prefers to get straight to the fact of the matter.

"Let us have the details."

Subba Rao clears his throat, pulls out a sheaf of papers from a folder, and hands it to Maruti Rao.

"A copy of *The New York Post* article that is to be published tomorrow. Chandresh Rajan sent it for our information."

Maruti Rao quickly scans the sheets before passing them on to the chief minister. Silence prevails for a while as everyone waits for him to read through the piece. Although his expression remains impassive throughout, the slight shift in body language is telling.

Finally he looks up and remarks to Subba Rao.

"They've left Prasad and Kumudini with nowhere to hide. Meticulously and thoroughly taken them apart! This is bound to raise a stink back in the US financial markets too. And the highly placed source that they have cited—is that you by any chance?"

Subba Rao hastily shakes his head. "I've known Chandresh for almost a decade now, sir. I did share the goings on at the ground with him, but certainly nothing else. The article is an eye opener for me as well!"

The chief minister nods in response before getting back to reading the report. After a few moments of silence, Maruti Rao clears his throat before addressing the chief minister.

"Do you anticipate some kind of political fallout? The article is clearly meant to expose Kamineni's political connections and the money laundering that has been taking place in the name of foreign investment."

The chief minister ponders over his question.

"I don't think we can afford any kind of political fallout. And there are ways to explain away the political connections. I am sure you understand this very well, given your decades of experience in the government."

There is a pause before the chief minister addresses Subba Rao again.

"When did you say this piece was coming out?"

"Tomorrow, sir."

The chief minister turns to Maruti Rao.

"It is a good thing that this is an international publication. I guess we must be thankful for small mercies, Rao garu!"

Maruti nods in agreement.

The chief minister turns to Rashid.

"So, Rashid garu, what is the status on the draft report that I had requested?"

Rashid looks nervous.

"It is more or less ready, sir. I was planning to discuss it further with Subba Rao garu and Veena Mehra garu...then this matter came up."

The chief minister notices the exchange of glances between Subba Rao and Veena Mehra.

"Political expediency might limit our power but it does not completely negate it!"

That is as candid a statement that the chief minister could have made while acknowledging the blockade on legal action against the MFI bosses.

The chief minister continues to address them in a resolute tone.

"Given that your districts have been the most affected by the crisis and given your intimate knowledge of the whole issue, I would like you to work closely with Rashid on this. Maruti Garu will then hold discussions with the law ministry and other relevant experts to ensure that we do not hit any kind of legal roadblock."

It is apparent to Subba Rao and Veena that the chief minister has an ace up his sleeve. Meanwhile, Maruti Rao can sense the questions racing through their minds and smiles to himself. He is only too aware of the chief minister's penchant for drama, how he likes to milk a situation for what it is worth before revealing any information he has.

"Should we go ahead and share our plans with them, Maruti Garu?"

Maruti Rao nods his assent, silently acknowledging the courtesy extended to him.

With an expression of utmost earnestness, the CM addresses his officials.

"The Government of Andhra Pradesh intends to promulgate an ordinance to regulate microfinance institutions. Every MFI in the state shall be mandated to register itself with the authorities in the districts of its operations. Henceforth, each of their transactions will come under scrutiny and will need to be cleared by the authorities. MFIs that use coercive methods of recovery will be made to face the music and violators will be imprisoned. No longer will the sector be allowed to fleece the poor of this state in the name of commercial microfinance, inclusive growth or any of the other pretty jargon that they've been peddling!"

Subba Rao and Veena exchange glances. Every single transaction? In the last couple of years alone, the top six MFIs in the state had disbursed a mindboggling 3.7 billion US dollars to as many as 30 million clients. They probably still have outstanding loans worth over 2 billion dollars in their collective kitty. The sheer volume of transactions that would come under scrutiny was staggering, to say the least!

"So, what do you think? We've got them on their knees, haven't we?"

Veena would have chosen a more colourful expression but for present company. She looks at MR but his expression is inscrutable. She wonders if he is thinking what she is.

Does this mean the end of the microfinance sector in its present form? Is it really Game Over for the Kaminenis, Kumudinis and their ilk?

EPILOGUE

PADERU VILLAGE, VISAKHAPATNAM DISTRICT,
23 AUGUST 2011

"They're back!"

Chandresh stares blankly at the laptop screen. He has typed one measly line in the last hour. His deadline is just a few hours away, and he is still struggling with the direction his article needs to take.

Chandresh had been working on a story on the challenge posed by the Maoists to the state, and has travelled to districts in Madhya Pradesh, Chhattisgarh and finally Andhra Pradesh. The editor of one of the papers he writes for had called him and specifically requested him to do a story on the microfinance sector in the aftermath of the Andhra Pradesh MFI Moneylending Ordinance 2010. Chandresh had been one of those who had strongly endorsed the ordinance in the belief that it would put an end to the impunity with which the MFIs had gone after increased profit margins and investments at the cost of the lives of the very clients they had pledged to serve. The article he had written along with Bob had earned him the ire of the microfinance sector bosses, who had considered it to be the trigger for the enactment of the ordinance. On his part, Chandresh knew it would be both presumptuous and juvenile if he actually bought into the view. The ordinance may have followed soon after the article, but the legislation had already been a long time coming.

And yet, what a travesty it had all turned out to be!

Chandresh stares moodily at his computer screen as he recalls the elation that he had felt following *The New York Post* article. It seemed that Kamineni and his ilk stood completely exposed. There had been political repercussions that went beyond the ordinance. There was an uproar in the parliament over the matter and Nageshwara Reddy had been forced to resign. Prasad Kamineni too had been made to quit the SAMMAAN board. When Chandresh's sources informed him that the IPO plans of a couple of other MFIs, including Kumudini's DevEx, had been indefinitely postponed, he had felt most gratified. It seemed that justice had been served. Nothing could make up for the lives lost but maybe their efforts would at least prevent further attempts at subverting the financial inclusion agenda and deriving extraordinary benefits from the disadvantaged and the poor. The stringent provisions of the ordinance and the increased state control and monitoring of the microfinance sector had effectively choked ground level operations. In all, it seemed that stories like that of Mylaram Kavala were a thing of the past.

The ordinance had also received the overwhelming

support of the political classes—always eager to position themselves as champions of the poor, who formed the bulk of their vote bank. Enthused by the bureaucratic and political support, many of the poor clients flatly refused to repay their outstanding loans; some even turned violent with the collection agents. It was a delayed response to the exploitative practices adopted by the MFIs. However, they had not been ready to face the consequences of their actions. The outstanding loans, default history and poor credit rating made them unworthy in the eyes of credit bureaus. As a consequence, the millions of poor in Andhra Pradesh, whom the ordinance had hoped to protect, had ended up having defaulter labels stuck on them and found themselves completely excluded from the ambit of formal credit.

"The moneylenders are back! They are back again!"

This had been the refrain on the ground during his recent travels across the state. The poor had had to turn, yet again, to informal sources, and the much reviled moneylender made a triumphant return. In essence, all the combined efforts of the past had ended up driving the poor into the clutches of the very forces that they had sought to rescue them from. They were back to where they had been—or perhaps, they were even worse off, for their hopes had been built up in the interim, only to be belied. They had lost faith in the system that only seemed to push them further into an abyss of despair and exploitation. The knights in shining armour had turned out to be knaves and their trust and confidence had been shattered.

The information that Chandresh received a short while

ago only served to corrode any remnants of confidence in the system and hope for justice.

Realizing that he is not going to get any work done in the black mood that he is presently in, Chandresh decides to step out for a smoke.

He strolls over to the tea shop across from the hotel. After asking for a cup of strong tea, he lights up and takes a deep puff on his cigarette. His eyes are drawn to the bench by the side of the shop and he recalls his meeting with the old Maoist during his last visit. It feels almost like another lifetime now.

He vividly recalls the flash of anger in the old man's eyes as he spoke of his landlord and his exploitative ways. The larger problem had remained: the lack of equitable access to resources had been the bane of the poor then and remained so now. The oppressors, like shape shifters, merely changed in form over time. Given the lack of access to education and resources, the poor continued to be at the mercy of these forces in their various forms.

As Chandresh stares moodily at the bench that he had shared with the old Maoist, his phone rings. Bob's voice booms into his ear.

"Hey Chan, I have some real good news for you!"

In his current sluggish frame of mind, Chandresh cannot think of a single reason for cheer.

"Hello Bob, good to hear you're in such high spirits. I sure could use some cheering up right now!"

"Chan, is everything alright? Is there a problem? Anything I can do to help?"

Chandresh smiles in spite of himself.

"Nothing more than a bout of professional blues, Bob. But go on...spill the beans?"

"I have just the news to dispel the blues, Chan. Our story has been nominated for the Simpson prize in the best investigative report category!"

Chandresh is not sure how to respond. Little does Bob know, he just added to his dark mood.

"Oh really...I suppose that is a good thing then."

There is a pause as Bob possibly tries to process Chandresh's unenthusiastic response.

"Chan, what is going on?"

"Nothing much, Bob. In fact, nothing at all. The sector's activities in the state have come to a grinding halt. The poor are being excluded by formal financial institutions all over again, and, guess what, the oppressive, usurious informal moneylender is back in business."

There is another pause—this time Bob is at a loss for words.

"I wouldn't go so far as to say that our report made this happen—that would make me delusional—but I am left wondering what we...I mean, what our report has really achieved. Like an old man once told me: You probably get paid well for your efforts and maybe even get some awards. But that's not much comfort for the people whose miseries you bare in print."

Chandresh closes his eyes, fighting against the tears of impotent rage that threaten to spill out.

"Chan, I assume you are referring to Nageshwara Reddy making an entry back into your central Cabinet. The gross illegality of transactions we exposed, the wilful attempts to subvert due process, all of it was made to bite the dust in the face of political expediency! Believe me, this is hardly the first time I have seen my efforts serve no great purpose."

Chandresh laughs dryly.

"You haven't heard it all, Bob. There is more good news in store."

Chandresh can almost hear Bob's mind racing as he speculates on Chandresh's words.

He takes a deep breath before he delivers the coup de grace.

"SAMMAAN and DevEx have both been granted banking licenses. They've been reinstated with greater powers and glory so they can have another go at their aborted agendas. It's business as usual for Kamineni, Kumudini and their brethren, Bob! Long live truth and justice!"

ABOUT THE AUTHOR

Ramesh S Arunachalam wears many hats. In the last two decades, he has been a columnist (with the *Hindu Business Line* and *Moneylife*), an entrepreneur, a filmmaker and also a development practitioner working on issues pertaining to financial inclusion and livelihood security. His clients include both state and national governments, bi-lateral and multi-lateral agencies, and the private sector in countries across Asia, Africa, North America and Europe.

www.ingramcontent.com/pod-product-compliance
Lightning Source LLC
Chambersburg PA
CBHW021037130626
46552CB00005B/1884